ELEPHANT FOR RENT

ELEPHANT

BY LUCILLE

Little, Brown and Company

Illustrated by Don Sibley

FOR RENT

CHAPLAN

Boston, Toronto

To My Friend Robin

CONTENTS

ELEPHANT FOR RENT

Chapter One. THE PRESENT

WHEN Jimmy McLean's father went to Africa to buy wild animals for circuses, Jimmy wanted to go with him.

"Not this year," Mr. McLean said.

"But I can help you!" said Jimmy. "I helped you look after the animals you brought home last year, didn't I?"

"You're very good with the animals — better than some men!" Mr. McLean agreed. "But it's a rough trip, and you're still too young. In a couple more years . . . well, we'll see!"

In the past, Jimmy had stayed with his grandmother while his father was away, but this year his grandmother was visiting some friends in California. So Mr. McLean left Jimmy with some people called Mudge, because they said they liked boys.

Jimmy soon found out, however, that they had not told the truth.

Mrs. Mudge had a sharp chin and untidy hair. She was always saying, "Keep off my clean floors. I don't want to sweep them again! Keep off my clean carpets! Keep off my clean chairs! Keep off my clean beds!" She was too lazy to cook proper meals, so all they had to eat was oatmeal — hot oatmeal for breakfast, and cold oatmeal for dinner and supper.

Jimmy liked oatmeal, but not three times a day!

Mr. Mudge was a gardener. He was a fat man with no hair on his head but a great deal on his chest and arms. He always wore his shirt sleeves rolled up and his vest and shirt unbuttoned, and his face got red whenever he shouted. His face was red most of the time. "Keep off that grass!" he would shout. "I just cut it! Keep off that gravel — I just raked it! If you touch those flowers . . ."

Poor Jimmy couldn't play in the house and he couldn't play in the yard. Since all his friends were away for the summer holidays, it looked as though he would have a very unhappy summer.

July 12 was Jimmy's birthday. Mrs. Mudge knew that it was his birthday, but she didn't do anything about it. No party, no presents, no cake — not even a "Happy Birthday, Jimmy!" Only the usual oatmeal, hot for breakfast and cold for lunch. But just as they were finishing lunch, the telephone rang, and it was for Jimmy.

"It's the stationmaster, Jimmy!" said the voice on the telephone. "Happy Birthday!"

Jimmy was surprised. He had spoken to the stationmaster several times, but he didn't know him very well. "How did you know it was my birthday?" he asked.

"Because there's a present here for you."

"Down at the station? What is it?" asked Jimmy. "Who is it from?"

"It's from your Dad," said the stationmaster, laughing at some private joke. "But I won't tell you what it is, and I'll bet you'll never guess. Come down and see!"

All the way down to the station, Jimmy tried to guess. He thought of all the things he had ever wanted — a cowboy suit, a real bow and arrows, a football — or could it be something *big*, like a bicycle? But his Dad was in Africa. Did they have bicycles in Africa?

He rushed through the station door, and then stopped suddenly. The stationmaster had been right: none of Jimmy's guesses were even close. There, by the ticket window, stood his present. It was looking at him. Attached to the present's collar was a big tag that read:

Happy Birthday, Jimmy
With Love from Dad

Jimmy took a step forward, and reached towards his present — and the present stretched out its trunk towards him! It was an elephant, a live baby elephant, with a rope tied to its collar so Jimmy could lead it home.

Now, Jimmy had always wanted a pet, and had often asked his Dad for one. He had dreamed of having white mice, or rabbits, or a puppy, or a pony — but a baby elephant was nicer than all the others put together!

"I told you that you'd be surprised," said the station-

master, grinning. "What are you going to call him? Tiny?"

"I — I don't know!" said Jimmy. Of course the little elephant must have a name. Not Tiny — that was silly; but — what? He had often thought of names for rabbits or white mice, but none of them seemed *big* enough for an elephant. One of the dog names might do — if the elephant liked it, of course. Spot? No, it was all gray. Rover, maybe?

"Here, Rover!" Jimmy called, but the little elephant paid no attention. Would he like "Rex" better? Rex was a *strong* sort of name. "Here, Rex! Come on, boy!" he called, and the little elephant came right to him. Rex had chosen his name.

"Good boy, Rex!" said Jimmy, patting the elephant's trunk. After thanking the stationmaster for calling him, he led Rex through the door and down the street towards home. Several people stopped him to ask what he was doing with the elephant. One little girl wanted to know if he was a parade! Jimmy explained that Rex was his pet, a birthday present from his father, and the people went away again, all except the little girl. She followed him for six or seven blocks to make sure he wasn't a parade.

When they got home, Mrs. Mudge said, "An elephant! And who is going to look after it, I should like to know? Mudge and I have enough to do."

"I can look after him," Jimmy told her. "Dad brought

home three elephants last year, and I helped take care of them all."

"And where is he going to sleep? Under your bed?"

"In the garage," said Jimmy. "We have no car."

"My bicycle is in the garage!" bellowed Mr. Mudge.

"Rex won't touch the bike," promised Jimmy, "and if you let him stay there, I'll polish your bike every week, and I'll keep the tires pumped up!"

Mrs. Mudge watched them start down the driveway towards the garage. "I warn you!" she called. "Don't expect me to cook enough oatmeal for *him!*"

Chapter Two.   THE MAN WITH
THE WHIP

FROM the day of Rex's coming, Jimmy saw the Mudges only at meals. All the rest of the day he was too busy. Every morning he worked, and every afternoon he played with Rex.

In the mornings he ran errands and swept the floor for Mr. Elliott at the Feed and Seed store. In return, Mr. Elliott gave him all the food Rex could eat, but it was a good thing that Jimmy had taken care of elephants before. Mr. Elliott knew all about horses, and cows, and baby chicks, but he didn't know *what* to feed an elephant.

At twelve o'clock Jimmy would hurry home, running most of the way. That wasn't because he was hungry for cold oatmeal but because he knew that Rex was waiting for him. Most afternoons they played in the deserted schoolyard.

Rex soon learned many tricks. He would pick Jimmy up, and carry him on his back, and open and shut the gate — that was his favorite trick. He understood everything Jimmy told him, and he usually did just as he was told. But when he got tired of tricks, he sometimes picked Jimmy up by the leg and held him upside down until he said — "All right! No more work! Let me down, Rex!" Then Rex would set him gently on the ground again, and the people who were watching through the fence would laugh.

There were usually people watching through the fence. Jimmy and Rex became quite used to passers-by stopping and watching. Sometimes quite a crowd would collect, and then Rex would put on his very best show. He liked having an audience! But with the exception of one very dirty, small child who lived nearby and came to watch them every afternoon, the audience was different each day.

The first time the man with the whip was there, Jimmy hardly noticed him. But the next day he was there again, and again the day after that. The fourth day, Jimmy watched for him but hoped he wouldn't come. There was something about him that made Jimmy feel uncomfortable.

"I don't know why he keeps coming," Jimmy told Rex. "I suppose he likes to watch us, but if he does, why doesn't he ever smile? And when you were bad yesterday and held me upside down, he looked so fierce, and tapped his boot with that whip he always carries. Everybody else laughed. I hope he stays away — Oh, here he comes now!"

All that afternoon the man watched them. Other people came and went, but he stayed; and when Jimmy and Rex left the schoolyard, the man was waiting outside the gate. He wanted to know to whom Rex belonged.

"He's mine!" Jimmy said. "My father sent him to me for a birthday present."

"Had him long?" the man asked.

"Two weeks and four days," Jimmy told him. "Why?"

"Bet you're pretty tired of him by this time," the man said. "An elephant! Silly present for a kid, anyway. I'll do you a favor, if you like, and take him off your hands. Give you a good price for him."

"My father isn't silly," said Jimmy. "Rex is the nicest present in the world, and I won't ever get tired of him. I won't sell him, either!"

The man looked at the ground and tapped his whip against his boot. "Don't get excited!" he said. "I just wanted to do you a favor. I thought you might be able to use a brand-new bicycle — a racer."

Jimmy laughed. "Rex is more fun than six bicycles!" he said.

"A bicycle and a pair of skates?"

"I'll never sell Rex!" Jimmy told him. "Now, let us by, please. We'll be late for supper."

The man let them pass, but the next day he was back again. "A bicycle, skates, *and* boxing gloves?" he offered. And when Jimmy said "No," he added an air rifle.

"If you don't go away," Jimmy told him at last, "I'll call a policeman! Rex is mine and I'll never, never sell him!"

This time the man went away and didn't come back. The next day Jimmy watched for him but he didn't come, and Jimmy and Rex had a fine afternoon without him — so fine that they forgot the time. It was quite late when they started for home, and Jimmy was worried about what Mrs. Mudge would say.

"The cold oatmeal won't get any colder," he told Rex, "but we'd better hurry anyway. Mr. Mudge will probably yell at us, too." Then, as they turned the corner — "That's funny!" he said. "Who's that going away from the house? Are those riding boots he's wearing? Oh dear, there's Mrs. Mudge at the door. She must be waiting for us!"

Mrs. Mudge *was* standing in the doorway, but when they came close enough to see her face, Jimmy hardly recognized it. Mrs. Mudge was smiling! And when she spoke, her voice was as new as her face — a sirupy, sweet voice that Jimmy had never heard before.

"Here you are, dear child!" she said. "I thought you would never come, and your lovely lamb chops, that Mudge ran all the way to the store for, getting stone-cold — never mind. I'll heat them up for you!"

"Lamb chops!" said Jimmy, so surprised that he forgot to watch where Rex was going.

"Hey!" roared Mr. Mudge, charging around the corner. "Get — that — elephant — off — my — lawn — or — I'll —"

"Mudge!" shouted his wife. Mr. Mudge stopped short

in the middle of a roar. His face got redder and redder until it was almost purple and he clenched and unclenched his fists, but he didn't say another word.

"That's right!" said Mrs. Mudge in her new voice. "Maybe the poor little elephant would like some fresh greens. Pick some of those new carrots for him, Jimmy, and a few of the hollyhocks. Mudge will help you." And Mr. Mudge did!

Chapter Three. THE STRANGE ACTIONS OF MRS. MUDGE

J IMMY didn't know what to think about the change in the Mudges — he only knew that he liked it! The supper *was* lamb chops, and very good, too. Breakfast next morning was bacon and eggs and toast and cocoa, with no oatmeal at all. Jimmy ate so much that he was sure he wouldn't need any lunch, but when he smelled the lunch, he hoped Mrs. Mudge would have second helpings of everything for him — and she did!

After lunch Mrs. Mudge said: "Now, run along, Jimmy. Take your little elephant out for his exercise. You must work up an appetite for supper, you know!" Jimmy and Rex went to the schoolyard as usual, but it was still quite early when they started for home. Jimmy couldn't wait to find out which would be waiting, the old Mrs. Mudge or the new one!

It was the new one. Again, she made Mr. Mudge offer Rex some of his hollyhocks, but Jimmy wasn't sure that hollyhocks would be good for elephants. They were never fed hollyhocks at the circus.

"But we must give him *something!*" said Mrs. Mudge. "A little treat. Look — I bought some breakfast cereals to-day. How would he like some Puffed Wheat?" Jimmy knew that wheat was grain, and elephants ate grain. He was just about to say "All right!" when Rex stuck his trunk into the top of the opened cereal box, sucked up half the cereal, and blew it into his mouth with a "whoosh!" He considered the taste for a moment, then reached in for the rest.

"There!" said Mrs. Mudge. "I'll buy him another box tomorrow. Now come along, dear child, your supper is waiting. Do you bolt the garage doors at night?"

"Oh, no!" Jimmy told her. "Rex can open doors, but he won't if I tell him not to. Be a good boy, Rex. Stay here."

The supper was a good one, with ice cream for dessert. Mrs. Mudge let Jimmy go down to the store to pick his favorite flavor, and he had two helpings. Perhaps he ate too much, because he woke up in the middle of the night with a stomach-ache. The Mudges were still up — he could hear voices downstairs. If Mrs. Mudge was still being nice, she might give him something that would make him feel better. Stepping into his slippers, he went out into the hall to call her.

From the top of the stairs, Jimmy could hear the voices in the living room. There were *three* voices, and when he heard the third one, he didn't call Mrs. Mudge. He even forgot that he had a stomach-ache.

First Mrs. Mudge spoke, and then Mr. Mudge, and then someone else. Mrs. Mudge answered. Then the third voice spoke again — and Jimmy was almost sure he knew who it was. Moving softly in his slippers, he crept down the four steps to the landing and peered through the banisters into the living room. He could see only the stranger's back, but that was enough. It was the man in the boots, the man with the whip — the one who had tried to buy Rex!

He was speaking now — and Jimmy, listening, was horrified to hear, "Why can't I take the elephant tonight?"

Mrs. Mudge answered in her old, cross voice. "You'll have to wait!" she said. "I told you that yesterday. I don't see why you want the horrid brute at all, let alone in such a hurry!"

"That's my business!" growled the man. "I'm paying enough for it!"

"If you're willing to pay so much," said Mrs. Mudge, "why bother with this one? Not that he isn't extra smart!" she added hastily. "Aren't there places that sell elephants?"

"Sure there are — but they won't sell to me!" growled the man. "They say I'm *cruel* to the brutes. Just because my last three died — was it my fault they couldn't stand proper discipline? Maybe I'll do better with this one. He'd be smart enough, if he weren't so spoiled."

"I'll bet you'll soon whip him into shape!" snickered Mr. Mudge.

The man slapped his boot with his whip. "That's my

business!" he said. "Now, how about it? Here's the money —"

"I'll take it!" said Mrs. Mudge.

"When I get the elephant you'll take it. Tonight?"

"It's not safe yet!" said Mrs. Mudge impatiently. "In another couple of days, we'll have the stupid boy thinking we're his best friends. Then he'll believe us when we tell him that the brute opened the door himself and ran away! Tomorrow I'm baking cookies — gingerbread. And Mudge, *you'll* make a kite tomorrow — a big one!"

Jimmy didn't wait to hear any more. He tiptoed back to his room and softly closed the door.

So *that* was why Mr. and Mrs. Mudge were pretending to be so sweet! Well, it wouldn't do them any good. If they thought they could fool Jimmy, and give Rex to the cruel man with the whip, they would find that they were mistaken.

"I'll lock the garage!" Jimmy thought. "No, that won't do. They might steal the key, or even break the door down. Well, they won't get Rex away from me! We'll run away, together, and stay away until Dad comes home, that's what we'll do!"

Of course he couldn't leave until the Mudges were asleep. In the meantime, he emptied his tin bank (he had six dollars and forty-seven cents) and got dressed. Then he heard the front door close — the man with the whip was leaving. The sound of footsteps on the stairs made him jump into bed, shoes and all, and pretend to be asleep. He was just in time.

His bedroom door opened, and through his almost closed eyelids he could see Mrs. Mudge standing in the doorway. "Yes, he's asleep!" she said softly. "Puffed Wheat! Gingerbread! Bah!" and she closed the door again.

When the house was quiet, Jimmy peered out into the hall. He could hear snores from the Mudges' bedroom, one high and one low. Now, if only the garage doors didn't creak when he opened them . . .

The doors did creak. The noise was so loud that Jimmy waited in horror for lights to go on all over the neighborhood and heads to poke through windows and shout: "What's going on down there?"

Holding his breath, he listened. That loud thumping noise—oh, that was his heart! There was no other sound but the crickets, much louder than usual, and the rustling, welcoming noises of Rex inside the garage.

Rex picked Jimmy up and they were on their way. Now, if only they didn't meet anyone they knew . . . Perhaps he should disguise himself? But that wouldn't be much use, unless he could disguise Rex too, and that might be hard to manage. They would just have to take a chance.

Chapter Four. FLIGHT

THE church clock chimed three. As Rex plodded along the silent street, Jimmy realized that he needn't have worried about being recognized, because the whole town was asleep. Even downtown, where he had expected to see lighted store windows and crowds of grownups, the streets were deserted and only dim night lights burned in the stores. Rex and Jimmy walked along with their changing shadows — a shadow boy on a shadow elephant, who swelled to monstrous size, then shrank again as they approached the next lamppost.

"Hurry, Rex!" said Jimmy. "We have to be a long way off by morning! Mr. Mudge will chase us on his bicycle, and he can ride fast!" They had passed through the downtown section by now and were on the outskirts of town. Again the crickets were loud all around them, but suddenly a red eye glared and a roaring, clattering monster bore down on them — and passed them.

"A train!" said Jimmy. "If we were on that, Rex, Mr. Mudge would never catch us!" Another train went by, this time a long, chugging one with many boxcars. It seemed to be stopping, and Jimmy realized that they were near the freight yards. "A train!" he said. "I wonder . . . Come on, Rex!"

One end of the freight yard was busy with moving lanterns carried by men who called to each other as they moved from car to car near the front of the train. Jimmy and Rex turned towards the other end of the train, far down the yard. It was dark there, with no lanterns and no streetlights nearby, but Rex seemed to see quite well. He picked his way carefully along the cindery, weed-grown tracks, and soon Jimmy's eyes became accustomed to the darkness too. At the very end of the train, he found what he was looking for — a boxcar with the door open, and luckily it was by a loading platform.

The car was empty except for a pile of hay at one end. It was darker in the car than outside — you couldn't see the stars, but the hay was soft to sit on. Jimmy yawned and stretched. "We should be safe now, Rex," he said. "What's the matter? Do you hear something?"

Rex was moving restlessly, so Jimmy went to the doorway and looked out. Sure enough, two lanterns were coming towards them. Jimmy and Rex moved back in the car as the men's footsteps crunched close. Outside their car, the footsteps stopped.

"This one empty, Bill?" said one of the men.

"Sure — nothing there but some hay."

"Want to pitch it out? We've still got time." The lantern moved close to the open door, and Jimmy and Rex tried to flatten themselves against the wall of the car.

"Aw — why bother? If we pick up some cattle later, we'll need it — here, give me a hand with this door." The lantern moved back, the door scraped and groaned shut, and Jimmy and Rex were alone in the sweet, hay-smelling darkness. A few minutes later the car jerked backwards, then forwards, and the train began to move. Rex trembled, but Jimmy patted his trunk.

"We're safe now, Rex," he said. "There's nothing to be afraid of. They'll never find us now, no matter how fast Mr. Mudge rides his bicycle." He laughed. "I'd like to see his face when he finds out we're gone!" He yawned and stretched again. "This hay is soft, but it tickles. I'll just shut my eyes for a couple of minutes. . . ."

When he woke up, Jimmy wondered who was rocking his bed. He turned his head, and something tickled the back of his neck. Then Rex snorted behind him, and Jimmy remembered where he was.

The night was over. Light shone through all the cracks in the car, and the rocking and jolting told him that they were moving farther and farther away from the Mudges and the man with the whip. He turned to see whether Rex was awake — and laughed. Rex was not only awake, he was eating his breakfast, and Jimmy turned to him just in time to receive an armful of hay the elephant thrust at him.

"No, thank you," said Jimmy, handing it back to him. "It's your breakfast. I don't like hay. Maybe it would be a good thing if I did, though. I'm hungry. The very first time the train stops, I'll slip out and buy something. I hope it stops soon."

But the train didn't stop. Hour after hour, it roared and rocked along. A few times it slowed down and Jimmy thought it was going to stop, but always it picked up speed again and clattered on. Jimmy dozed, and woke, and dozed again. Rex ate more hay, and Jimmy got hungrier and thirstier every minute and wondered whether the train was ever going to stop. Well, of course it would have to stop sometime, but it might go on for a week first, or maybe longer! Maybe it will be a month! Jimmy thought. . . . He didn't say it aloud, because he didn't want to frighten Rex. . . . Maybe Rex and I will get thinner and thinner until we starve to death, and someday when they *do* stop and open the door, they'll find a boy skeleton and an elephant skeleton in the car, and wonder how they got there!

The light coming through the cracks wasn't so bright now, and still the train roared on. Earlier in the day Jimmy had talked to Rex about the Mudges, and what the man with the whip would say when he learned that Rex had escaped. Now, however, his throat was too dry to talk much and he just sat in the hay, his back against Rex's stout leg, and waited for the train to stop.

It was after dark before they slowed down again, but this time the train did not immediately pick up speed and roar on. It went slower and slower, and finally stopped. No lights shone through the cracks — the station, if there was one, must be away off at the other end of the train. Now all Jimmy had to do was open the door, and he and Rex could slip quietly out into the darkness. Nobody would ever know — but what was wrong with the door?

It was a sliding door, and Jimmy pushed at the edge, but it wouldn't slide. He pushed harder, but still it didn't move. He pushed with all his strength — and now he remembered: it had taken two men to close that door! Stepping back, he prepared to throw himself against the edge, even though it wouldn't do any good, but just as he braced himself, light gleamed through one of the cracks.

Jimmy held his breath and listened. Yes, footsteps were approaching, and there were more gleams from moving lanterns. Then he heard voices.

"This it?" asked the first voice.

"No, the next one." The footsteps crunched closer. The men were talking quietly, and then Jimmy heard, "Nonstop to the Coast, huh?"

"That's right," said the first voice. "Wish I were on this train. I've got a brother in California. Give me a hand here!" The lanterns were very close now, and there was a rattling sound at the front of the car, but Jimmy wasn't worrying about rattling sounds.

"Nonstop" the man had said. That meant that if Jimmy and Rex didn't get out right away, there would almost certainly be a couple of skeletons on board by the time the train got to California! If only he could make the men hear, they would let him out, but his throat was so dry . . . Maybe if he banged on the door — after all, even going back to the Mudges was better than starving to death!

He raised both fists to pound on the door — and then he remembered. If he went back to the Mudges, the man with the whip would get Rex. In silence, he listened to the retreating footsteps of the men who might have let him out.

"Never mind, Rex!" he whispered. "We may starve, but at least we're together. Oh my gosh, what a dope I've been! Here, Rex — you're strong enough to open this door! *Push,* boy!"

Rex lumbered forward, but just as he began to push, the train whistle blew. Once more they heard the familiar chugging. Slowly, steadily, the door creaked open, but

Jimmy sat on the floor of the car, his face buried in his hands.

"It's no use, Rex," he said. "We're heading nonstop for the Coast!"

Chapter Five.   APPLES

Rex gave the little trumpeting squeal that meant he had done his trick and was proud of himself, but Jimmy did not look up. "It's no use, boy," he said. "If only I had thought of you before!" Rex trumpeted again, and Jimmy roused himself. "All right," he said. "I'll come and look. It's not your fault that I was stupid."

As he moved towards the opened door, he half-noticed that the car wasn't rocking as it usually did. The darkness outside didn't seem to be *moving*, either. And why did the engine's chugging sound so far away? He poked his head through the door and then leaned so far out that Rex caught the end of his coat to keep him from falling.

The train was moving. It was traveling fast — but they weren't going with it!

As he watched the light at the end of the train become a pin-point in the distance, Jimmy figured out what had happened. Those men who had been working around the car — that clanking sound — they must have been uncoupling it. After all, why should they take an empty car all the way to the Coast?

Now their car stood alone on a spur of deserted, weed-grown track. In the darkness, Jimmy could make out other car shapes on other tracks, and in the distance a small lighted building, probably some sort of station. The coast was clear.

Moments later, their car really was empty. Jimmy and Rex, an elephant shadow with a boy shadow on its neck, were trudging along a moonlit country road.

They were hungry and thirsty, but the night air felt good after the stuffy boxcar. Once, as they passed a farm-house, a watchdog barked at them. The barking sounded frighteningly loud in the quiet night.

A little later, Rex began to move faster and tried to leave the road.

"Rex!" said Jimmy. "Straight ahead!" Rex shook his head in protest, but did as he was told. A moment later the soft thudding of his footsteps in the dirt changed to a hollow thumping. They were crossing a little bridge. Below, Jimmy could hear the gurgling sound of —

"Water! Is that what you were trying to tell me? Come on, Rex!" Slipping and scrambling, they made their way down to the stream. First they drank and drank, then Jimmy washed his dusty face and hands. Rex must have felt dusty too, or perhaps he just liked playing with the water. At any rate, he poured trunkful after trunkful over his head and back until Jimmy made him come away, and by that time he was so wet that Jimmy couldn't ride, but had to walk along beside him until the night breeze had dried his back.

They walked, and then they rested. By the time they started out again it was beginning to get light, and Jimmy saw his first sunrise. The sky was still pink with it when they came to something that looked prettier to Jimmy than any sunrise. It was an apple orchard!

When he bit into his first apple and the sweet juice ran down his throat, Jimmy decided that he had never in his life tasted anything so good. He handed one to Rex, but Rex had already helped himself. Jimmy was just finishing his second apple, and Rex was reaching for his fourth when they heard:

"Hey there! Boy!"

They turned around. It was a farmer.

"Run, Rex!" said Jimmy, vaulting onto the elephant's back. A running elephant covers ground fast, and they would have left the farmer far behind if he hadn't called:

"Stop, boy! I won't hurt you! I want to talk to you!"

A little uncertain, Jimmy told Rex to stop. "I hope he's not too mad," he said. But when the farmer came puffing up, he was laughing.

"Never chased an elephant before!" he panted. "Never thought I'd have to!" He stopped to catch his breath, then said, "I didn't mean to scare you when I yelled. Just wanted to tell you that you're welcome to all the apples

you can eat. I'm going to lose most of them anyway."

"I'll bet I can eat twenty-five of them right now," said Jimmy. "Thanks a lot!"

The farmer laughed again. "I like apples too, but twenty-five could give you an awful stomach-ache. Why don't you have some breakfast with me first, and then eat apples?"

"Rex too?" asked Jimmy.

"Is that the elephant's name? Of course. Rex too!"

When Rex was settled in the barn with a good meal, the farmer took Jimmy to the house where breakfast was waiting. Instead of twenty-five apples, Jimmy ate nine pancakes with plenty of sausages and applesauce and three glasses of fresh milk.

"Now *that's* the kind of an appetite I like to feed," said Mrs. Dixon, the farmer's wife. "Will you have another sausage?"

Jimmy drew a deep breath. "I'm afraid I couldn't!" he said. "Thanks, anyway!"

"Some apples?" suggested Mr. Dixon with a grin.

"Not even one apple!" Jimmy told him. "Say, Mr. Dixon — why did you say you were going to lose all those apples? Is someone going to take them away from you?"

Mrs. Dixon answered. "Just the opposite," she said. "We're going to lose them because *nobody* will take them away from us!"

Jimmy looked puzzled, and farmer Dixon laughed. Then he explained: "We can't get anyone to help us pick them.

Most of the apples will rot before the two of us can get around to them."

Jimmy thought fast. "Would you like to hire a strong boy?" he asked. "A strong boy, and a very strong elephant?"

Chapter Six. A HIRED ELEPHANT

JIMMY had worked before, but it was the first time Rex had ever had a job. Mr. Dixon thought it was very funny to have an elephant working for him. "I've had hired men and hired boys," he said, "but this is the first time I've ever had a hired elephant!"

Right after breakfast they went out to the orchard. Mrs. Dixon didn't think an elephant would be much help in apple picking, but she soon changed her mind when she saw him work. Jimmy showed him how to pick an apple, put it gently in a basket, and then pick another, and soon he was working faster than anyone else. After all, he just stood on the ground and picked — he didn't have to climb ladders with empty baskets and down again with full ones. His basket wasn't always as full as it should have been, however, because every now and then Rex would stop and have a little snack!

At noon, Jimmy and the Dixons ate the picnic lunch Mrs. Dixon had brought. Rex was so full of apples that he didn't want any more — for a little while. Instead of eating, he taught himself a new trick, which he practiced happily until Jimmy saw what he was doing and stopped him. Rex had discovered that if he grasped a branch with his trunk, and shook that branch very hard, all the apples would come bumping down!

In the afternoon they picked again, and that night Jimmy slept in the little upstairs room which had been Mr. Dixon's when he was young. It had a slanting roof and a small bed with a patchwork quilt, and on the wall hung a bow and a quiver of arrows made by Mr. Dixon himself many years ago, when he was just a small boy named Willie.

Every morning for the next week, Jimmy and Mr. Dixon hurried through the early chores while Mrs. Dixon made breakfast and packed the lunch basket. After breakfast, Jimmy would bring Rex from the barn and they would all go to the orchard.

By the end of the second day, Rex had picked all the apples he could reach, but Jimmy found plenty of other work for him to do. For one thing, he made a wonderful ladder. Imagine a ladder that would come when it was called, lift you into a tree basket and all, and then come and lift you down — or take your full basket away and bring you an empty one! Rex couldn't lift Mr. Dixon, and Mrs. Dixon wanted to stay on the ground, but he took away their full baskets, and brought them empty ones, and carried the regular ladder wherever it was needed. Rex was the busiest elephant who ever picked apples!

By the end of the week, all the apples that were to be shipped were on their way, and Mrs. Dixon had several carefully packed barrels stored away for her own use. None were left but the windfalls to be picked up and sorted. The best were put aside for cider, and the badly bruised ones were given to the pigs, who grunted and snorted and ate all they could get, bruised or not.

Although Jimmy was a little tired of apples by this time, he was sorry the job was over. Now he and Rex would have to be moving on — but where? At breakfast the next morning, he asked: "Will it be all right if we stay till the afternoon, Mr. Dixon? I promised Rex he could help feed the pigs again. He likes to watch them."

Mrs. Dixon stood still, a spoonful of batter halfway to the skillet.

"Must you go?" she asked. "Mr. Dixon and I were hoping you would stay with us for a while. Don't you like it here? Have another pancake!"

Jimmy looked at Mr. Dixon, who nodded. "As long as you want to stay," he said, "you're welcome!"

With a happy sigh, Jimmy poured sirup over the pancakes Mrs. Dixon had piled on his plate. "We'd love to stay!" he said. "What do we do today? What comes after the apples?"

Mr. Dixon's eyes twinkled but his face was serious. "I have something in mind," he said, "but I'm not sure you can handle it."

"I'll bet we can!" Jimmy said. "Why?"

"Can you swim?" asked Mr. Dixon.

Jimmy was surprised. "Sure!" he said. "Why?"

"Have you ever been across the north field, on the other side of the orchard?"

"Yes," said Jimmy, puzzled. "There's a creek there. But —"

"Well," Mr. Dixon began solemnly, "I want you to follow that creek —"

But Mrs. Dixon interrupted him.

"Don't tease the boy!" she said, laughing. "There's a swimming hole, Jimmy, about a quarter of a mile down the creek, and I have a lunch packed for you. We thought it was about time you had a day off."

Jimmy pushed his plate away. Suddenly he was full. "Oh boy!" he said. "I can teach Rex to swim — if the swimming hole is big enough! Rex has the day off too, doesn't he?"

"Of course!" said Mrs. Dixon. "Rex has earned his holiday too. And I think the swimming hole is plenty big enough. It's deep, too. You be careful, Jimmy. And see that Rex is careful, too!"

It was a perfect day for swimming, hot, but with a little breeze. It was a perfect day for anything — anything outdoors! Rex seemed to be happy too, and Jimmy let him amble along, stopping whenever he wished to sample some tender grass. Jimmy was walking barefoot, proud of the toughness of his feet — until he stepped right into a patch of thistles.

As they wandered towards the swimming hole, Jimmy explained to Rex about swimming. "I'm not sure *how* an elephant swims!" he said. "*I* lie flat on the water, and wave my legs and arms, and always breathe in with my mouth and out through my nose so I never get a noseful." He laughed and patted Rex's trunk. "I guess you wouldn't have to worry about that, would you, Rex? . . . Where are you going?"

Rex had broken into a lumbering run, and he paid no attention to Jimmy's calls of "Stop, Rex! Wait —"

And then Jimmy heard it too, and stopped shouting and started running himself. It had been a gurgling cry of "Help! Help! He-elp!"

Chapter Seven. RESCUE

Rex burst through some bushes and disappeared from sight. When Jimmy followed, he found himself in a clearing where the creek had been dammed to make a good-sized swimming hole. On the grass lay a little pile of clothes and a lunchbag like Jimmy's own, but there was nobody there — not even Rex! Where had he gone? Then Jimmy spied Rex's head, halfway across the swimming hole!

"Rex!" called Jimmy. "Come back here!" But Rex paid no attention.

Jimmy was just about to plunge in after him when he saw Rex stop, lower his trunk into the water, and a moment later turn and head for the shore again dragging something. No, it was some*one!* It was a boy!

As Rex laid the boy gently on the grass, Jimmy tried to remember what he knew about artificial respiration. He was just going to send Rex for help, when the boy opened his eyes and then quickly closed them again.

"Are you all right?" asked Jimmy.

With his eyes tight shut, the boy answered, "Maybe

I'm dead! I don't feel too bad, but I thought I saw an elephant!"

Jimmy laughed, and the boy opened his eyes again.

"*You* look real enough," he said, propping himself on his elbows. "But is that really an elephant?"

Jimmy introduced Rex, who offered his trunk to be patted. Then the boy said, "Where did you two come from, anyway? And how did I get out of the water? The last thing I remember —"

"Rex pulled you out," Jimmy explained. "Are you sure you're all right? Do you want — a drink of water or something?"

The boy made a face. "Have a heart!" he said. "I just swallowed half the pool! I'm all right, but if I'm ever such a dope again . . . You're a dope, Bill Gibson!" he told himself sourly.

Jimmy laughed and sat down beside him on the grass. "What did you do?" he asked.

"I got a cramp," Bill said. "I asked for a cramp, and I got it. If my mother ever finds out . . ." Jimmy still looked puzzled, so Bill explained. "I went swimming right after a nice, big breakfast. Those pancakes alone were enough to sink me! Say, can Rex do tricks? Can he sit up and beg?"

"That's a dog's trick!" said Jimmy. "Rex can do better than that. Come on, Rex, let's show him!" They showed Bill all the tricks except the apple-picking and door-opening ones — there were no apples and no doors to open!

Then Bill wanted a ride, so Rex carried him around and around the clearing. On the fifth time around, he called down to Jimmy, "Are you visiting around here?"

"No, we're working!" said Jimmy. "We came on a train, and we had our own private car!"

"How come?" Bill slid off Rex's back and joined Jimmy in the grass. While Jimmy told Bill about their adventures so far, Rex wandered about the clearing, sampling the tender leaves and grasses that grew near the water. Soon he got tired of that and wanted the boys to play with him, but Jimmy had just got to the place in his story where the man said: "Nonstop to the Coast!"

"Gosh, what happened *then?*" asked Bill, and then, "What does Rex want?"

"He wants to play. Later, Rex. We're busy now. Go away!"

Rex went, but only as far as the edge of the pool. There he filled his trunk with water, turned — and sprayed the water full in Jimmy's face!

"Rex!" sputtered Jimmy. "You bad elephant! I'll — I'll — Stop laughing, Bill Gibson!"

Bill was rocking back and forth, his arms clasped tight across his stomach. He could hardly talk. "I can't — help it!" he gasped. "You looked so funny — so surprised — Oh!" The playful elephant had done the same thing to him!

Dripping, Bill jumped to his feet. "You'll pay for that, Rex! Come on, Jimmy, let's duck him!" They chased the elephant into the water, Jimmy shedding his clothes as he ran. They tried to duck Rex, but he was too strong for them. He broke free and backed away, spraying them as he went with trunkful after trunkful of water. By the time they caught him again, they had forgotten all about the ducking and tried to climb up on his back instead.

Rex let them climb on, then dumped them off! After that they played King of the Castle — Jimmy stood on Rex's back and Bill tried to pull him off, then Jimmy tried to pull Bill off, then Rex threw them both off and they tried again to duck him.

By that time Jimmy and Bill were hungry, so they came out of the water and ate their lunches while the sun baked them dry. After lunch they rested and talked and wrestled in the soft grass. Bill was stronger but Jimmy was more wiry and could always wiggle free before Bill pinned him down.

Later, they used Rex for a diving platform. He let them jump off his back, but each time they disappeared under water, he pulled them out and dragged them all the way to shore.

"He must think he's a lifeguard!" grumbled Bill, coming back into the water for the third time.

Jimmy laughed. "We were pretty glad he *was* a lifeguard a little while ago. Hey, where are you going?" Bill had swum once around the pool and now was on the bank again, pulling on his trousers.

"Chores!" he said. "Look at those shadows. It's late!"

Jimmy came out and dressed too. "I didn't notice," he said. "The Dixons will be looking for us, too. See you next week?"

"Wednesday, if I can make it. Meet you here." At the beginning of the path, he turned. "We'll duck that elephant next time!" he said.

Rex made a trumpeting noise that sounded very much like a laugh.

Chapter Eight.   A WARNING

B Y THE end of the month, Jimmy had decided that he and Rex would have a farm of their own someday. Oh, he still planned to go to Africa with his Dad, but they would work it out somehow. In the meantime, the more he learned about farm life, the more he liked it, and Rex seemed to like it too.

Of course, Rex had to be watched or he got into trouble. Once he did his favorite gate-opening trick and let all the goats into Mrs. Dixon's flower garden. And the time he nearly drowned forty baby chicks, by spraying a whole pail of water over them, Jimmy was afraid they would be asked to leave. Was it just mischief, or did Rex think he was giving the chickens a drink? There was no way of finding out.

But when all the hay had to be brought in before a storm broke, Mr. Dixon said that Rex did more work than a hired man and a team of horses. All working together, they beat the storm, and that night Jimmy lay in his cozy attic bed, and listened to the rain drumming on the roof right over his head. It was a restful sound, especially when he thought of all the hay safely under cover, but he hoped it would stop before morning. Tomorrow was Wednesday, and he and Bill had big plans for the whole day. For a long time, he lay dozing and thinking of their plans — and then suddenly he was wide awake and listening in the darkness.

Listening for what? There wasn't a sound, not even the rain — that was it! Jimmy smiled and relaxed. The rain had stopped. But suddenly a rattling burst of sound made him sit up in bed. A short silence; then it came again, rattling against his window. Hail?

Sliding out of bed, Jimmy ran to the window and looked out. The rain had stopped. Below, in the moonlit yard, stood Bill, his arm raised to throw another handful of gravel at Jimmy's window. When he saw Jimmy, he called in a hoarse whisper, "Jimmy! Come on down! Hurry!"

Jimmy slipped through the back door and joined him. "What's the idea?" he asked. "I was going to be at the swimming hole in the morning. Wouldn't your Dad give you the day off?"

"I'll be there all right," said Bill. *"But I don't think you'd better be!"*

Jimmy stared at his friend. "What do you mean?" he asked.

"I came to warn you!" said Bill. "Do you know two men on bicycles? The fat one is bald but he has a regular doormat on his chest, and the other one wears riding boots and carries —"

"A whip!" said Jimmy. "Of course I know them. They're Mr. Mudge and the man who tried to get Rex! Where did you see them?"

"At my house," said Bill. "The fat one told my mother they were looking for his little boy —"

"*His* boy!" exclaimed Jimmy.

"That's what he said. *His* boy, who stole his friend's elephant! Hey! Where are you going? Wait for me!"

Jimmy was running towards the stable. "Rex!" he said. "Maybe they've got him already!" But Rex was still there. When Jimmy opened the stable door, Rex opened one eye and then closed it again. By that time Bill was there too. "I could have told you he was all right!" he panted.

Jimmy was tugging at Rex's leg. "Come on, sleepy!" he begged. "Wake up! We've got to get away — fast!"

"Take it easy," Bill said. "You've got all night. They won't be here till sometime tomorrow."

Jimmy turned to face him. "Are you sure?"

"Sure I'm sure!" said Bill.

"How do you know?"

Bill grinned. "They can't start until they pump up their tires. They got — kind of flat, somehow. All four of them. And they might have trouble finding a pump. I think I did a pretty good job of hiding it —"

Jimmy felt a little better. "Where are they now?" he asked.

"At my house, asleep in the spare room. It was late and

raining when they rode up, so of course Mom invited them to stay the night —"

"Didn't your mother tell them that I was right over here?"

Bill grinned again. "She doesn't know," he said. "I didn't tell her anything about meeting you at the swimming hole. I like secrets. Besides —"

"Besides what?"

"My Mom's like a detective. If I told her one single thing, she'd find out everything about my nearly drowning, and I wouldn't get another chance to swim this summer! What are you and Rex going to do now?"

Jimmy was sitting on an old box, his chin on his fist. "I don't know!" he said. "Start running, I guess. But once they really start chasing us on those bicycles — maybe we should just stay here. I'm *not* his little boy, and Rex is *my* elephant."

Bill looked worried. "Who's going to believe that, when two grownups say you're lying?" he asked. Jimmy didn't answer, and Rex, who was wide awake now, moved over and rested his trunk gently on Jimmy's shoulder.

"A council of war!" Bill said. "That's what we need! Light the stable lantern, Jimmy, and shut the door. The three of us are going to have a meeting!"

In the friendly glow of the lantern, things looked more hopeful and Jimmy's numbed brain began to work. "Hey!" he said. "What if I write a note before I go?"

"What kind of note?"

"A note that says where I'm going!"

Bill stared at him, and Rex watched them both. "That's crazy!" Bill said. "Then they'll go right there and find you!"

Jimmy grinned. "Not if I go somewhere else!" he said.

For a moment longer, Bill stared. Then, "Oh, boy!" he said "A pencil — I think I have one in my pocket — here. It's kind of chewed, but I think it'll write. Paper — paper — paper — is that a paper bag over there? Put it on that box for a table — now, where *don't* you want to go?"

They spoiled the first half of the bag, but they finished the note on the second half. "There!" said Bill, climbing up on Rex's back. "Read it out, Jimmy, and see how it sounds."

Moving close to the lantern, Jimmy read their scrawling pencil marks:

DEAR MRS. DIXON:

GOOD-BY. REX AND I ARE TIRED OF BEING FARMERS. WE ARE GOING TO NEW YORK. THERE ARE BIG SHOWS IN NEW YORK AND MAYBE REX CAN GET IN ONE. THANKS FOR ALL THE DINNERS AND EVERYTHING.

YOURS TRULY,

REX AND JIMMY MCLEAN

"That sounds all right," said Bill, sliding down and giving Rex's trunk a farewell pat. "Now, I've got to get go-

ing. If Mom ever finds out I've been out at night —
Wow!"

"Wait'll I blow out the lantern!" said Jimmy. "There!"

Bill opened the door. "See you sometime!" he said.
Then he melted into the darkness.

Chapter Nine. "I'VE GOT A GUN!"

THE country road was dark. In many places the trees met overhead, and Jimmy and Rex passed through black tunnels where Jimmy couldn't even see his own hand when he held it close to his face. Still Rex plodded on, advancing steadily. His big feet made plop-plopping noises in the mud, and sometimes he splashed through puddles left by the evening's rain.

Jogging along through the rain-washed darkness, Jimmy began to get a little sleepy. He was thinking of Mrs. Dixon and how she would find his note in the morning. First she would call him from the foot of the stairs. "Jimmy," she would call, "time to get up!" And maybe she would say, "If you don't hurry, Mr. Dixon will eat all the blueberry muffins!" When he didn't answer, she would climb the stairs, puffing a little, to laugh at him for being such a sleepyhead. And all she would find was an empty bed with a note on the pillow. . . .

Perhaps he shouldn't have run away. Mrs. Dixon liked him a lot, and the farm was swell, and there was Bill. He could still go back. No! Mr. Dixon liked them both, but

Mrs. Dixon didn't really care for Rex. She had been very surprised when Jimmy told her Rex was a birthday present. Now, when two grown-up men told her that Jimmy had *stolen* the elephant and he wasn't a birthday present at all . . .

"Hurry, Rex!" said Jimmy. "The sign at the crossroads said that New York was the other way, but — wait! What's that?" Rex stopped, and Jimmy peered into the darkness ahead. Were those lights? They were small red lights, two near the ground and two high above them. What were they doing out here? "Stand still, Rex. Wait for me!" ordered Jimmy. He slid from the elephant's back and crept forward to investigate.

At first he saw only the lights; then, as he advanced, a great bulk loomed behind them. Were the lights on a wall — a wall across the road? No, not quite *across* the road.

With a sudden, terrifying roar the thing sprang into life! Jimmy jumped back. Then, as lights shone somewhere ahead and big wheels churned the mud, he laughed.

It was only a truck, a big truck. If the driver was friendly, maybe he would . . . Just as Jimmy reached the end of the truck, the motor stopped and he heard a voice. Who was the driver talking to? Maybe this was a trap, a trap to catch him and Rex! Holding his breath, Jimmy listened.

The man was swearing. To make it worse, he seemed to be swearing at a lady! Jimmy didn't know whether he should run away or go ahead and see whether the lady needed rescuing. After only a moment's hesitation, however, he went forward, inching along the side of the truck as quietly as an Indian scout.

The driver was saying: "You're a lazy, useless, good-for-nothing —" Suddenly he stopped, drew a deep breath, and when he spoke again it was in a different tone. "All right, girl," he said soothingly. "Let's try *once* more. Come on, now. For me!" A match flared as he lit a cigarette, and Jimmy, who was now right beside him, saw that the man was alone.

Now the engine roared again. As the wheels slithered and spun in the grooves they had dug in the mud, the man shouted: "Come on, girl! Come on!" He was talking to the truck.

The engine was shut off. "No use, old girl!" said the driver. "Maybe in the morning we'll find a team of horses —"

"Would one elephant do?" asked Jimmy.

The truck driver whirled to face the window. "I've got a gun!" he cried. "Whoever said that, come out where I can see you. Keep your hands up, and no funny business!"

Jimmy came forward, his hands held high. When the truck driver saw him, he seemed angrier than ever.

"Where did *you* come from?" he asked. "Scaring the living daylights out of me — oh, for Pete's sake, put your hands down. I don't have any gun." After a look at Jimmy's face, he grinned. "Guess I scared you too. Sorry.

But that'll teach you to pop up in the middle of nowhere talking about elephants. Elephants!"

"But I have an elephant," said Jimmy. "If we help pull your truck out of the mud, will you give us a lift? Come here, Rex!" he called.

"Oh, sure!" said the driver. "And if that doesn't work, we'll try your helicopter — Hey! What's that? It's an *elephant!*"

"It's *Rex!*" said Jimmy, laughing at the driver's surprised face. "Shake hands, Rex!" Rex reached his trunk through the window of the truck, and after a moment's hesitation, the truck driver shook it. "Hi, Rex!" he said. "I'm Mike!" He looked at Jimmy. "Now, if this elephant is real" — he looked down at his hand — "he felt real — let's see what he can do!"

He climbed out of the cab, a flashlight in his hand. In the back of his truck he found some boards, and Jimmy helped him arrange them and some stones from the side of the road in front of the wheels. Then Mike climbed back into the cab and started the engine. Rex pressed his forehead to the back of the truck, and pushed. The wheels spun and caught the edge of the boards — Rex gave a mighty heave.

The truck climbed out of the rut and onto solid ground again.

By six o'clock, the time Mrs. Dixon would be reading Jimmy's note, the truck was rolling over the highway al-

most a hundred miles away, with Jimmy and Rex in the back. Jimmy had dozed for a while, but now he was wide awake, and Mike was explaining why he had pretended to have a gun.

"I'm carrying a valuable load," he said. "Furs. When I stopped for coffee last night, the boys were talking about some hijackers operating around here, holding up trucks. Well, we lost a load last month that way, so I thought it might be safer and quicker to take that short cut — short cut! I'd 'a' been there all night if you and the elephant hadn't come along. How far do you want to go?"

"As far as you're going!" said Jimmy. "We want to go a long, long way!"

Chapter Ten. DILLON'S DINER

MIKE said that he was glad to have company. "Gives me somebody to talk to besides the old lady, here!" he said, patting the truck's dashboard. "She listens to me all right, but she's not much on answers!"

Jimmy laughed. "Do you often give people lifts?" he asked.

Mike shook his head. "Company rule!" he said. "No passengers! The way I figure it, though, an elephant that pulls you out of the mud isn't really a *passenger*."

"Rex and I won't tell anybody," Jimmy promised. "So if you don't say anything about us, nobody will ever — What's the matter?"

Mike had slowed down, and was watching the road ahead with unusual care. "Accident ahead," he said.

Jimmy looked, but as far as he could see the road was clear. There wasn't even a car in sight. Of course there was no way of knowing what might be around the next bend, when the road curved like this. They rounded the bend, and there it was! At the side of the road was a small truck. Its front was jacked up, and a man in overalls was doing something to a wheel.

Mike stopped and leaned out the window. "Need any help?" he asked.

"It's just a tire," the man said. He straightened, and wiped his forehead with the back of his hand. "Thanks, anyway!"

"Okay!" said Mike. "Glad it's not worse!" He stepped on the gas, and when they were rolling along again, Jimmy asked, "How did you know something had happened around that corner?"

Mike grinned. "Radar!" he said. Then, "Didn't you notice the truck that passed us going the other way? He signaled with his lights that something was wrong on the road ahead. It's bad enough to have a flat. This way, at least your own buddies won't run you down while you're changing it. You getting hungry?"

"A little," Jimmy admitted.

"Me too. We'll stop soon."

Until Mike mentioned it, Jimmy hadn't realized how hungry he was. He began to watch for eating places. In the last hour or two they had passed at least a dozen, but now they drove and drove but there wasn't one in sight. At last, far ahead, he saw a big sign that said RESTAURANT. What would he order? He could begin with bacon and eggs and toast — lots of hot, buttery toast — but just as he got that far, Mike drove right past the restaurant!

Jimmy had already tasted that toast in his mind, and his mouth was watering. Perhaps Mike hadn't seen the restaurant? It seemed a long time before another place came in sight — a sign that said SNACK BAR beside some overnight cabins. "Right there!" he told Mike, but Mike drove on.

"That's not the place," he said.

"You mean we're going to a special place?"

"Sure!" Mike must have sensed his surprise, because he added: "Most truckers have regular stops, places where they know the food is good. The one we're coming to has a couple of bunks in the back room. I hope they're not full!"

"Are you going to bed?" asked Jimmy.

"Just for a nap. After driving all night, I need it. When I have a truck line of my own, I'll have the big ones with a bunk in the back and two drivers, so one can sleep while the other one drives. There it is! Right up ahead!"

The sign said DILLON'S DINER. It was smaller than some of the places they had passed, and its green-and-white paint was a little shabby, but a number of trucks were parked in front of it. Mike drew up between a green panel truck and a big trailer transport.

Jimmy looked in on Rex and promised to bring him some breakfast, then he followed Mike through the diner's screen door. The blond lady behind the counter was saying, "You're late, Mike. Run into trouble?"

"Got stuck," Mike explained. "Any messages?"

She glanced at the blackboard that hung behind the cash register, then shook her head. "Nothing for you," she said. "If you want a bunk later, it's okay. I gotta call Bill in fifteen minutes. Now, what'll you have to eat?"

There were booths under the window, but all the truck drivers were at the counter, so Jimmy and Mike sat there too. Jimmy had bacon and eggs and toast and milk and French-fried potatoes and then some pie and ice cream. He was just thinking about a second piece of pie, and deciding that he didn't have room, when a young man in a checked shirt came through a door behind the counter. He was rubbing his eyes.

"Bunk's yours, Mike!" said the blond lady. To the young man she said, "Your boss called, Bill. You're to make an extra stop."

While Mike had his nap, Jimmy took a box of Puffed Wheat, some wiener buns, and half a dozen apples out to Rex. As they waited for Mike, the young man Bill drove away in the trailer transport and other cars and trucks came and went. Hidden in the back of Mike's truck, it was fun for Jimmy to listen to the drivers talking to each other and never guessing that a boy and an elephant might be listening. What they said wasn't very interesting, mostly just "Good-by" and "See you Thursday" and talk about roads and loads and traffic policemen. Jimmy must have dozed a little, because suddenly, close beside the truck, he heard a low and angry voice saying, ". . . stuck in the mud!"

A second voice answered, "Was that my fault? I didn't make it rain! We'll get him tonight! He always stops —" Doors slammed, and an engine roared. Jimmy thought sleepily, "A lot of cars must have been stuck last night." He looked out to see whether Mike was coming, and noticed that the green panel truck was gone. Just then the diner door opened. Jimmy ducked back out of sight — he didn't want anyone to wonder what a boy was doing in the back of a truck that was supposed to be locked — but it was only Mike. They were on their way again.

Chapter Eleven. A VALUABLE LOAD

MIKE was wide awake now and full of talk. As they rolled along, he told Jimmy all about his wife and their two children — both girls, but the older one was the best baseball player on the block. Jimmy was pretty sure he could play baseball better than any girl, but he didn't say so.

Mike talked a lot about his truck, too, "the old lady." She was a good old lady, he said, but she belonged to the company, and Mike was saving up to buy a truck of his own. With his own truck he could make more money, and then he could buy things for his girls. Right now, they wanted a bicycle and some roller skates. . . .

Jimmy thought of his own Dad. *He* had sent Rex to Jimmy, and Rex was nicer than any old bicycles or skates. If only he were home . . . But he wouldn't be home for three weeks or more. . . . Mike was still talking, but Jimmy found it harder and harder to keep his eyes open while he listened. Well, he could listen with his eyes closed! Suddenly, he and Rex were in the schoolyard at home. Rex was on roller skates, four of them. He offered to lend Jimmy a pair, but Jimmy wanted to borrow the ones from his front legs and Rex said Jimmy could only have them if he would wear them on his hands. So he put them on his hands. But when he tried to skate that way, he slipped — and nearly slid from the leather seat of the truck.

"That was quite a nap you had!" said Mike. "Look! I bought some sandwiches and things for lunch." They found a place where a big field ran down to a stream, and there they let Rex out for a run while they sat under a tree and ate their sandwiches.

On the road again, Mike became more and more cheerful. Tomorrow morning he would be home, and he was going to take his girls to the beach. Swimming! Jimmy remembered the fun he and Rex and Bill had had at the swimming hole. It seemed so long ago! They were far from the Dixon farm now — and far enough from the man with the whip, too. Perhaps one of the farms they were passing needed a boy and an elephant? He would ask Mike to let them off at the first place that looked promising.

They passed farm after farm. Some looked too small, and some were too big. Some were too shabby and untidy-looking, and a few were so full of tractors and jeeps and things that they wouldn't need an elephant. None of them looked nearly as nice as the Dixon farm, and suddenly it was suppertime and they had come to a place that served fried chicken but no forks — you used your fingers.

Rex had some supper and a pail of water, and they were on their way again. Once more Jimmy looked at farms, but he still hadn't found one that looked right when it grew dark. What should he do? In a few hours, Mike would be home, and he mustn't have passengers on his truck. If he and Rex got off now, maybe he . . .

"Oh-oh!" Mike put his foot on the brake.

"What is it?"

"Up ahead. Somebody in trouble. See?"

In the middle of the road, a man was waving a flashlight. His car was parked at the side, its headlights on. Mike stopped beside the man. "Need some help?" he asked.

"Engine conked out." The man turned his light once towards Mike and Jimmy, then put it out. "I think I know what the trouble is, though, and if you two could give me a hand —"

"Sure thing!" said Mike. As Mike drew the truck up on the shoulder of the road, Jimmy was trying to remember where he had heard the stranger's voice before. His car, too, seemed familiar. Mike's headlights showed that it was a green panel truck.

"Come on, Jimmy!" Mike was out of the truck already. "Now, what do you want us to do?" he asked the man with the flashlight. "Hey! What's the idea?"

"Keep 'em high and you won't get hurt!" The man now held a gun, so Jimmy and Mike put their hands in the air. "That's right!" said the man. "All right, Ed. Come and search 'em!"

From behind the truck, another man appeared. "Where did the kid come from?" he asked. "That makes two of them we've got to get rid of — stand still, you!" He was patting Mike's pockets. "No gun!" he reported.

"The keys, stupid. Get his keys."

Suddenly Jimmy remembered where he had heard those voices *and* seen the green panel truck. At the diner, of course! And they had been talking about a car that got stuck in the mud — why, he had heard them planning the robbery, and not had sense enough to tell Mike about it! Now Mike would lose his load of furs, and probably his job. Maybe they'd both be killed!

While the man with the flashlight and gun kept them covered, Ed had found the keys and started towards the back of the truck. Rex! What would they do to Rex? Would they kill him too, or would they sell him to somebody like the man with the whip?

"If we could only get his eye off us for a minute," Mike muttered, "we might be able to get that gun!"

Ed had been trying keys.

"There!" he said at last. "This is it! Now, let's see those lovely, lovely furs —" But as he turned the key in the lock, Jimmy called: "Rex! Help! Come quick!"

At the sound of "Help!" Rex charged through the truck doors, trumpeting. He bowled Ed over, and the man screamed as he fell. As the bandit with the gun swung around to see what was happening, Jimmy dived for his legs and Mike grabbed for his gun.

Ten minutes later, the bandits were tied hand and foot with ropes from their own truck, and Rex was stand-

ing guard over them *and* the furs they had tried to steal.

"And if you don't behave yourself," Jimmy said, "I'll tell my elephant to eat you!"

"Elephants don't eat people," muttered the gunman.

"Would you like him to sit on you, then?" laughed Mike.

"All right, all right," said the gunman. "Hauling elephants for bodyguards — that's — that's un-American! If I'd known we were hijacking this fur on the hoof —"

"Elephants don't have fur!" said Jimmy. "Guard them, Rex!"

On the road once more, Jimmy asked Mike, "What are you going to do with them?"

"Turn them over to the State Police," said Mike.

Police! Jimmy didn't want to go to a police station. The man with the whip probably had a notice out about a stolen elephant! If only Mike would let him out here — "Mike!" he said. "Stop! Rex and I get out here. Thanks for the lift — you've been swell."

Mike didn't want to let them go. He said that Jimmy and Rex deserved most of the credit for catching the hijackers. Jimmy insisted that he didn't want any credit. "And besides," he said, "what would your company say if they found out you were carrying passengers?"

Mike stopped the truck. "Well," he said. "If that's the way you want it!"

As Jimmy climbed out, he asked, "Do you think those fellows will talk about Rex?"

"If they do, I'll say they were dreaming. Nobody will believe them, anyway. But I don't think they'll want anybody to know they were caught by a kid and an elephant."

When Jimmy and Rex stood in the road, Mike leaned out the window to say, "Good luck!" Then the engine roared and he was off.

Jimmy and Rex watched the taillights of the truck disappear over the hill, and then they looked around them. The night was bright with moonlight, and in a field near the road they could see a haystack.

"Come on, Rex," said Jimmy. "I've always wanted to sleep in a haystack!"

Chapter Twelve. THE GAS STATION

Jimmy woke to the feeling that his pillow was sliding off the bed. Still half asleep, he tried to pull it back, but instead of cloth and feathers he grasped only hay — *moving* hay! As he raised his hand to investigate, the hay was whisked right out from under it! With a whole haystack to choose from, Rex had picked the tuft under Jimmy's head for his breakfast.

"Rex!" said Jimmy. "Someday I'll wake you that way and see how you like it!" With his mouth full of hay, Rex cocked his head on one side and looked at him. Jimmy laughed. How *could* he wake an elephant that way?

While Rex ate his breakfast, Jimmy brushed the hay from his hair and clothes and got rid of the tickling bits that had crept under his shirt. It was a cool, sparkling morning, just right for exploring and adventures. The road was waiting, and it might lead anywhere. "Come on, Rex!" said Jimmy. "Let's see what's over that hill. Wait! Do you hear music?"

For a moment they stood and listened. Then, when the summer breeze brought the thin, reedy strains again,

Jimmy and Rex followed. As they climbed the long steep slope of the hill, Jimmy wondered who would be making music so early in the morning, and away out here in the country. And what kind of music was it? Not a voice, or a violin. He was panting a little from the climb and the hurrying, when they reached the top of the hill and looked down on the other side.

They saw a long, gentle slope. Halfway down, a town began. But now the music was very close and Jimmy could see where it came from. Just over the crest of the hill was a small gas station, and on the bench in front of the white-painted shack sat a young man with the curliest red hair Jimmy had ever seen. He wore dark coveralls and a cap pushed far back on his head, and he was playing a harmonica.

When Jimmy and Rex came up, he raised one red eyebrow in a surprised but friendly fashion. He didn't stop playing until he reached the end of his tune, when he tapped the harmonica three times against the palm of his left hand, shoved it into his back pocket, and grinned.

"Hi!" he said. "My first customers today! You won't be needing gas or oil, I guess. How about some water?"

"Rex could use a drink," Jimmy said. "After all that hay —"

"Help yourself!" The young man waved his arm. "Pail right over there — tap around the side."

Jimmy took care of Rex, and when he came back he

found that the young man had spread wrapped sandwiches and pieces of fruit all over his bench and was gazing at them with sad blue eyes. A blue Thermos bottle stood by the bench.

"What's the matter?" asked Jimmy. His mouth was watering.

His eyes still on the food, the young man said, "My aunt is a remarkable woman!"

As Jimmy stared at him — the answer didn't seem to make sense at all — the young man continued, "I don't mind too much when she thinks I'm as *smart* as two people. I kind of like that. But when she gives me enough food for two people, and gets mad if I leave any of it . . ." He turned to Jimmy. "You couldn't help a fellow out, could you? Force yourself to eat something?"

Jimmy didn't have to force himself, and he didn't wait for a second invitation. They ate in friendly silence, broken only when the young man said things like, "Some more milk?" or, "I can recommend the egg sandwiches. I know the hen personally!" Several times his lunch was interrupted by customers. They all called him "Charley" and seemed to like him a lot.

When the fourth customer drove up, Jimmy looked at the pile of empty sandwich wrappings and decided that Charley's aunt wouldn't get mad at him this time. The fourth customer was a cross-looking man who kept telling Charley to hurry up, hurry up, he didn't have all day. Charley was just giving his windshield a quick wipe when

— splash! A stream of water hit the glass right in front of the customer's nose! Rex, with his pail of water, was either playing or trying to help!

The customer had been cross before. Now, for a moment, he was speechless, and in that moment Charley acted. Quickly drying the windshield with his polishing cloth, he tossed his cap onto Rex's head. "Have you met my new assistant, sir?" he asked the customer. "He washes, I wipe. Part of Charley's superservice — no extra charge for the only elephant car-wash in town!"

As the man drove away, laughing, Jimmy tried to apologize. "That's all right!" said Charley. "I've known Mr. Phelps for twenty years, and this is the first time I ever saw him smile. Rex deserves a medal, not a scolding. . . . What can we do for you, sir?"

The small man who had come limping over the hill looked hot and dusty. "Do you fix cars?" he asked.

"Yes, *sir!*" said Charley. "All you have to do is bring it in!"

"If I could do that it wouldn't need fixing," the small man said. "And I wouldn't have blisters on both heels from walking so far, either!"

"What happened?" Charley asked.

"I was just driving along — and then all of a sudden I wasn't. It stopped. You'll have to send your tow truck."

Charley pushed his cap still farther back and rubbed his head. "I have no truck," he said. "Maybe you can get a lift into town, and save your heels, but I just wish I could get your car in here. Wait a minute! Did you ever ride an elephant?"

"Gracious, no!" said the small man. "And I don't think I ever want —"

"Jimmy!" said Charley.

"Up, Rex!" said Jimmy.

"Oh, help!" said the small man. "Make him put me down! He doesn't *like* me!"

"He'll be all right if you'll please let go his ears!" said Jimmy. "All right, Charley, we'll bring in the car. Come on, Rex. Sit tight, sir!"

With the driver steering the car and Rex pushing, it didn't take them long to bring it into the station. Charley found the trouble at once — it was a loose connection. "There you are, sir!" he said, wiping the grease from his hands. "If you like our service, tell your friends about it!"

"Elephant tow service," said the small man. "My gracious, I certainly will tell people about it." As they watched him drive away, Charley said, "I knew this business needed something, and now I know what it is. An elephant! Now, if Rex were for sale, rent, or hire —"

"He is, if only you'll hire both of us!" said Jimmy eagerly. "I can do lots of things too. What's the matter? Did I say something wrong?"

Charley had whirled on his heel and was striding back toward his shack. Jimmy, running after him, saw him lift the receiver of the phone that hung on the wall. He heard him ask for a number, then say, "Aunt Ella? . . . Charley. Is your garage still empty? . . . Good. How about your spare bedroom? . . . Because I've finally hired some help, that's why. An unemployed elephant. . . . No, I said elephant. . . . No, no, not in your spare bedroom! In the garage. His boy goes in the spare room. Okay? . . . Thanks, Auntie, you're a doll. We'll see you at supper-time. No, we won't be late!"

Turning to Jimmy, who had been listening in amazement, he added: "I have a cap that may fit you, if it's not too big, and Auntie can cut down a pair of my coveralls. But tell me: do you think Rex needs a uniform?"

Chapter Thirteen. THE CHURCH BAZAAR

CHARLEY's aunt was little and quick. She met them at the door and immediately took charge of everything. "Come right this way and I'll show you to your room," she told Jimmy. "By the time you've washed up, supper will be ready. Charles Augustus Bain, keep out of my kitchen. There's nothing there for you!"

"I thought I smelled apple pie," said Charley. "Did you make me a pie today, Auntie?"

"If I did, it's more than you deserve!" his aunt told him severely. "Now, you take that nice little elephant out to the garage — I left some carrots and things there for him. He does eat carrots, doesn't he?" Jimmy nodded and would have spoken, but Aunt Ella was talking to Charley again. "After you get the elephant settled, come in and wash your hands, and then if you're *very* good, we'll see about the pie. But no dawdling, mind! Hurry up!"

"Yes, Auntie. Right away, Auntie!" said Charley, pretending to be frightened.

After dinner, Charley said, "It seems a pity to leave that

last quarter of a pie *sitting* there, but I just can't do any-thing about it! Well, back to work. Coming, Jimmy?"

"You're a greedy boy and I'm ashamed of you!" said Aunt Ella. "And Jimmy isn't going to the gas station to-night — he's coming with me! I have three cakes and a basket of cookies to take to the church bazaar, and I can't manage them *all* myself. Well — what are you waiting for? Get along to your gas station, and you might as well take that quarter of a pie with you. It's only cluttering up my kitchen!"

On the way to the bazaar, Aunt Ella explained: "We're holding this bazaar to raise money to send two crippled kid-dies to the city for hospital treatment. I hope we make enough! The pony rides should help. All the children have been saving their nickels for weeks, and Mr. Eldridge is bringing both his ponies. . . . Oh, dear, what's the mat-ter *now?*"

A crowd of ladies had burst through the church gate just as Jimmy and Aunt Ella approached. Now they sur-rounded Aunt Ella, all talking at once.

"Please!" said Aunt Ella. "One at a time!"

There was a moment's silence, then they all began again. "Bessie, you tell me!" commanded Aunt Ella.

The very plump lady in the flowery dress must have been Bessie. "Ella Bain!" she said. "You don't have to be so *calm* about it! Seventeen children are waiting for the pony ride, and more coming every minute — and there aren't going to be any ponies!"

"No ponies?"

"That's right!" A tall thin lady in a straight black dress chimed in. "Mr. Eldridge just phoned that one of his ponies has a split hoof, and the other got hurt when his youngest boy was playing cowboy and tried to jump the pony over a hedge after some rustlers."

"That's Teddy Eldridge, isn't it? Was he hurt?" asked Aunt Ella.

"Oh, no —he landed on his head, and those Eldridges have the *thickest* heads. But the pony was hurt —"

"And now all those children are waiting to ride a pony that isn't coming!" The plump lady was wringing her hands, and all the other ladies started talking again.

Jimmy touched Aunt Ella's sleeve, and she glanced at him and nodded her head. "Rex!" she said. Jimmy set down his baskets and started to run back toward the house. Behind him, he heard Aunt Ella say, "Really, of all the things to get excited about! If we can't have ponies, we'll just get an elephant!"

By the time Jimmy got back with Rex, a black crayoned sign that said PONY RIDES 5¢ was lying on the ground, and a new sign in red and black crayon was being put up. The new sign said ELEPHANT RIDE 5¢, and there were at least twenty-five children waiting under it.

Rex brought in more nickels than any two ponies could have done. In fact, he brought in more money than any booth except the cake sale. A man with a flash camera took some pictures and said, "See tomorrow's paper!" and the children all came back and brought more children, and Jimmy wouldn't have had time to see the rest of the bazaar at all if Aunt Ella hadn't hurried up with a blond, freckled boy just about Jimmy's size.

"This is Teddy Eldridge!" she announced. "He runs his father's pony rides sometimes, so he can take care of Rex while you have a cold drink and look around!"

"Sure I can!" said Teddy. "Hi, Rex!"

Jimmy had a drink and some ice cream, and then tried the dart game.

He broke two balloons with three darts, and won a harmonica, and he was just going to try his luck again when he heard Teddy calling, "Hey, Jimmy! Help! Rex! Put me down!"

Rex was holding Teddy upside down. Jimmy rescued him, stopped Rex from picking the colored light bulbs (he must have thought they were apples), and then it was time to go home.

Chapter Fourteen. TIGERS AND KANGAROOS

AFTER Jimmy's late night at the bazaar, Aunt Ella wouldn't let Charley wake him, and it was nearly ten o'clock when he and Rex hurried up to the gas station.

"Sorry we're late!" panted Jimmy. "We'll make up the time! What shall we do first?"

"Sit down," suggested Charley, who was sprawled comfortably on a bench. "At least, *you* sit down. I don't suppose Rex wants to."

Still ready for action, Jimmy asked, "Isn't there *something* we could do?"

Charley considered. "Well," he said, "I suppose we could sell gas to each other. But I have all the gas I want, and you don't need any. What's this I hear about your winning a harmonica? Can you play, 'There's a Long, Long Trail A-Winding'?"

"I can't play anything very well," said Jimmy.

"Time you learned, then!" said Charley. "Here! Let's see how you hold it."

They had almost half an hour of practice before a customer came, and as he drove away, two more came in. Jimmy had helped with all three, and now he asked, "When can I take one myself?"

"Take this fellow coming in now," said Charley. He flopped down on the bench and looked up at the sky, whistling. Jimmy hadn't expected to be left on his own quite so soon, but he filled the gas tank, wiped the windshield, and said, "That will be three seventy-eight, sir. . . . Change for *twenty* dollars?" He looked to Charley, but Charley was still whistling softly to the sky. Well, he wouldn't *ask* for help. Figuring in his head as he ran, he hurried to the shack for change. For the first time in his life he was grateful for all the mental arithmetic drills he had had to do in school.

As the customer drove away, Charley stood up and stretched. "Nice work," he said. "You take this car, now, and I'll take the truck — Hey, Rex!"

"No, Rex!" shouted Jimmy.

They were just in time. Left with nothing to do, Rex had turned the tap and filled his water bucket. Now he was just raising his trunk to "wash" a car window — and the window was open! After that, they kept closer watch over him, and kept him busy polishing windshields (with a dry cloth!) and carrying things and towing. Between jobs, they let him pick up cigarette packages and other papers dropped by customers.

In the middle of the afternoon there was a lull, and

Charley said, "How about going over that 'Long Long Trail' again? It still sounds pretty bumpy to me." Jimmy was about to take out his harmonica when he glanced down the road. "Hey!" he said. "What's that cloud of dust? It doesn't look like a car — oh, it's bicycles! There must be a dozen of them! Is it a race?"

Pedaling furiously, the leading bicycle reached the service station, turned sharply in, and headed straight for Jimmy. Inches from him it skidded to a stop and a black-haired boy jumped down. "Tiger!" he shouted. "You're a Tiger! Don't forget."

"Kangaroo!" The second bicycle had arrived. It was Teddy Eldridge, the boy from the church bazaar. "He's a Kangaroo!" shouted Teddy. "I knew him first, Speed Gilbert, and I say — " By this time Jimmy and Rex were surrounded by boys shouting "Tiger!" and "Kangaroo!"

The black-haired boy calmed them down. "Quiet!" he shouted. "Qui-et! Jimmy doesn't even know us yet! We're two baseball teams, Jimmy, and we're each a man short, and we play back of Charley's station here, and we're in the middle of a big series, and — "

"And we want you to play with us," Teddy finished for him. "He's the Tiger captain, and my team is the Kangaroos. I saw you throw those darts last night. I'll bet you're a good pitcher. How about it?"

"Swell!" said Jimmy, then — "I'd love to. Only, Rex and I *work* here. We don't have time — "

Now it was Charley who was surrounded. "Aw, Charley!" . . . "You've gotta let them play!" . . . "Charley's a good guy!" . . . "Don't be a stinker, Charley!"

"All right, all right!" Charley raised his hands in surrender. "Time off for fire, flood, and baseball practice. Now clear out of here and make room for some customers."

Whooping and yelling, they poured out of the gas station and raced down the road towards town. But one of them turned and came flying back. "Sorry, Charley. Almost forgot!" he panted, thrusting a folded newspaper into Charley's hand and pedaling off after the rest of the crowd.

Jimmy followed the retreating bicycles with his eyes. "Thanks, Charley," he said. "It was nice of you —" But just then Charley gave a long, low whistle and said "Look at this!"

Right across the front page of the paper was the headline *ELEPHANT AIDS CHURCH BAZAAR*. And the picture showed Rex with three children on his back. "Hey, Rex! Look at this!" called Jimmy.

"We'll be busy tonight!" said Charley. "Talk about advertising! Everyone in town will see this!"

"I don't see what that picture has to do with gas," said Jimmy.

"You will!" said Charley.

And Jimmy did. From suppertime on, car after car

drove out from town for gas. Each car was filled with children who wanted to see the elephant.

Jimmy dreamed that night that Rex had turned into a striped Kangaroo; and instead of pushing cars, he was carrying them in his pocket.

Chapter Fifteen.   BASEBALL AND C.S.S.

THE next morning, Jimmy woke to find a regular pair of dark coveralls, just his size, at the foot of the bed. On the pocket were red letters that said C.S.S., for Charley's Service Station. There were also two caps, one marked REX in large gold-embroidered letters. When he tried to thank Aunt Ella, she said, "There's nothing to *thank* me for! I'm just trying to keep your clothes clean and save myself some work!" She looked very fierce, but she didn't fool Jimmy. The new cap didn't keep his clothes clean, and neither did Rex's cap, which she had fixed with an elastic to hold it on.

The Tigers and Kangaroos played baseball in the big field behind the gas station, and Jimmy and Rex played with them. Jimmy was a Kangaroo. The Tigers had gotten another boy who had just returned from a summer trip. Rex wasn't a regular member of either team. They had tried him out, but even though he could sometimes hit the ball, he wasn't good enough for serious games.

"And these games are *serious!*" Teddy Eldridge said. "Do you know what the winning team gets?"

"What?" asked Jimmy.

"Free passes for the Saturday afternoon show, that's what!" said Teddy. "It's my uncle's show. And after the show, free sodas! Speed's cousin runs the ice-cream place. So we can't take Rex on one of the teams. I hope he doesn't mind."

They finally decided to make Rex batboy and water-boy for both teams. Since the Tigers wore yellow caps for a uniform and the Kangaroos wore red, Aunt Ella sewed red and yellow ribbons to his gas station cap. The teams didn't really need a batboy, but Rex made a very useful waterboy. He would carry his bucket to the gas station, fill it, and bring it back — and if they were hot, he was always glad to give them a shower.

Whenever Charley needed help, he blew three notes on his harmonica and Jimmy and Rex came running. But he needed most of his help early in the evening, when the cars full of children came out to ride Rex and see him do tricks while their fathers bought gas. The trouble was, Jimmy was so busy with Rex and the children that he didn't have time to fill gas tanks. At last Charley said, "How about it, Jimmy? Couldn't you find a trusty Kangaroo to lead Rex around and play ringmaster?"

"I'll try!" said Jimmy.

When he asked for volunteers the next day, the whole team wanted the job — and so did all the Tigers. "Rex is a Tiger just as much as he is a Kangaroo!" they said. It was finally decided that one Tiger and one Kangaroo should be on duty each night as Official Elephant Trainers.

Several times a week the teams played ball. At first nobody came out to watch the games except a few little brothers and sisters. But as the series went on, and first one team led and then the other, fathers and older brothers began to show up.

The series called for fifteen games. By the time the series stood at 7-7, everyone in town was interested. So many people wanted to watch the final game that they decided to have it in the evening. And then — greatest glory of all — the *high-school athletic coach* offered to umpire for them!

Almost everybody in town turned out to watch this final game, even Aunt Ella, who had never seen a baseball game before. But she cheered, and waved her straw hat, and shouted, "Come on, Jimmy, get that goal!" and seemed to be having a wonderful time. And when Rex trotted over to the gas station for water, he came back with a big basket full of bottles of soft drinks. The basket was labeled:

For My Animal Helpers — Tigers, Kangaroos, and Elephant

The Kangaroos got the first two runs, but in the third inning Speed hit a homer with the bases loaded, and after that the Kangaroos couldn't seem to bring a man in. As they were going into the second half of the ninth, Speed

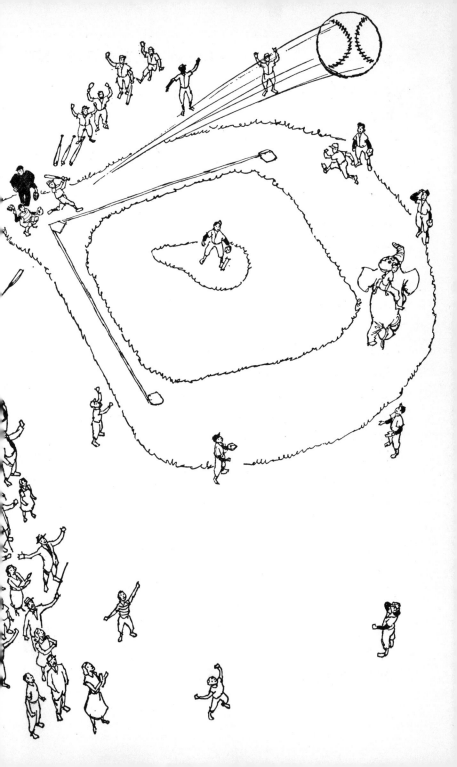

stopped Teddy as he was coming in from the pitcher's box.

"Say, do me a favor?" he said.

"What kind of favor?" asked Teddy warily.

"Tell your uncle I'd like a western for my free show."

Teddy grinned. "Tell him yourself — if you win!" he said. Then he stepped up to the plate and hit a line drive that got him to second base. The next man got to first — and the next two struck out. Then a boy named Phil slid safely into first, but twisted his ankle doing it.

As the team gathered around, Phil got to his feet, tried to walk, and sat down again, holding the ankle. Two of the boys helped him to the side, and the umpire said, "You'd better put in a substitute to run for him."

"We only have one substitute," said Teddy doubtfully.

"That's all right. Trot him out!" said the umpire. Teddy whistled. "Here, Rex!" he called. "Jimmy, you coach him!"

"Maybe I'd better ride him!" said Jimmy. "Is there any rule about that, Mr. Umpire?"

The umpire rubbed his chin. "I doubt it," he said. "I'm quite sure the question has never come up before."

So Rex ran with Jimmy on his back, and a thin boy named Sam, who had struck out four times, hit the ball halfway to the gas station for a home run.

The Kangaroos won the series, eight games to seven, and Rex carried Phil home on his back, because that ankle was still pretty sore.

Chapter Sixteen.   VICTORY DAY

ON SATURDAY, the Kangaroos held their victory parade. Led by Rex, who wore his cap, a red rug on
his back, and a gold-colored bathrobe cord looped around
his neck, they marched all the way down Main Street to
the movie theater. Jimmy rode on Rex's back, playing
"There's a Long, Long Trail A-Winding" on his harmonica as loud as he could; and all along the way, people
came out of their houses and stores to see them.

When they got to the show, Teddy's uncle came out to
meet them and led them right up to the door, past all the
line of boys and girls waiting for tickets. An usher took
Rex away to spend the afternoon with his friend, the
baker's horse.

The show was a double feature, a cowboy picture and a
dog picture, and there were three cartoons and a serial.
After the show, they went to the ice-cream store and all
had free Super-Duper-Sundae-Specials, the most expensive
thing on the menu. When they left, they were given a big
bag of peanuts and three bananas for Rex.

After supper that night — he was too full of his Super-Duper-Sundae-Special to eat much — Jimmy was ready to start for the gas station; but Charley said, "Didn't you know? Some of the fathers are giving a big roast tonight for both teams!"

It was a wiener and marshmallow roast, and all the Tigers and Kangaroos were there. They sharpened sticks for the wieners and marshmallows, and there was plenty for everybody, even though Rex found the food baskets and ate a dozen rolls and half a pound of marshmallows before he was caught.

When there was nothing left to eat they sang songs, and then somebody said, "I know a ghost story!" So they told ghost stories.

Speed told one about a haunted house. He spoke very low, and they had to lean forward to hear. "There was this man who didn't believe in ghosts!" he said. "So they dared him to spend a night alone in a haunted house. And just at midnight a bony hand touched his shoulder, and a ghostly voice said in his ear —"

"Hi, fellows! Having fun?"

The boys were so startled that some of them nearly jumped into the fire. "Charley!" said Jimmy. "You scared us!"

"Sorry!" said Charley. "Must be these rubber-soled shoes. What was it — ghost stories? Do you know the one about the headless horseman?" He squatted down between Jimmy and Phil and told the story in a low, thrilling voice.

It was a good story — it ended with the horseman galloping through the night, his head, which was tucked under his arm, shrieking horrible curses at the man who had killed him.

The last embers of the fire were winking out when he finished, and suddenly everyone realized that it was late. But nobody felt like leaving. Not if it meant going off in the darkness, alone.

All together, they stamped out the last sparks and kicked dirt over them to make sure they were out. Then the whole crowd walked Teddy home — his house was nearest. From there, they went around the corner to drop Phil off, and then the next boy, and the one who lived nearest to him. At last only Jimmy and Charley and Rex were left, and it was after eleven o'clock.

Jimmy shut Rex in the garage and fastened the door from the outside so he wouldn't get into mischief during the night. Then he joined Charley at the back door and they tiptoed up the stairs. Aunt Ella was already asleep.

When Jimmy climbed into bed, his mind was whirling with the parade, and the show and the sundaes, and the roast, and the stories. "I'm not even tired!" he thought — and then he was asleep. But either the stories had been too good or he had eaten too many hot dogs and things, because he had a horrible nightmare. A Thing was chasing him through the night — an awful Thing. It kept gaining and gaining on him, and his feet were so heavy he could hardly lift them. It was right behind him, and he tried to scream and couldn't, and just as a bony hand reached out and touched his shoulder — he woke.

He woke trembling and as wet with perspiration as though he really had been running. For a few minutes he lay still and listened to the pounding of his heart, and then, as the pounding subsided, he looked around the room. It was no longer pitch-dark — he could see the bulky shapes of the furniture, and through the window the sky was still dark but the stars had faded.

It was then that he heard the engine. It was a heavy engine — it sounded like a big truck, and very close. Maybe right in front of the house. But what was a big truck doing on their quiet street, so far from the highway? And the driver was racing his motor. "Silly goop!" Jimmy thought. "That won't do his engine any good!"

The truck drove away at last, and Jimmy turned over and prepared to go to sleep again. But somehow, he couldn't settle down. His pillow was hot. He thumped it and turned it over. It felt better then, but his mind kept wondering about that truck. Of course, the driver might have been taking a short cut and lost his way. And he might have stopped to light a cigarette, or look at a map, or — almost anything!

This was silly. Practically the middle of the night, and he was wide awake. Maybe if he slipped out and talked to Rex for a little while, he would be able to get back to sleep.

Jimmy tiptoed down the stairs and slipped the latch of the back door. Once outside, he almost turned around and went back. It was a silly hour to wake Rex. But when he looked towards the garage, he suddenly noticed that the doors were swinging open. He remembered closing those doors. . . .

"Rex!" he called in a loud whisper. "Rex! Come on out! Are you all right?" He ran towards the garage, but no Rex shuffled forward to greet him.

The garage was empty.

Chapter Seventeen.   MISSING

THE garage was empty. Jimmy stared into the gloom as though he expected the shadows to thicken and become a dark gray elephant, but nothing happened. Rex was not there.

Had he escaped? Perhaps he had somehow managed to get the door open. If the lock was bent, he would only have to push it — but even as he reached for the flashlight hanging on the garage wall, Jimmy knew that Rex had not opened that door. He wanted to believe that he had, but when the light showed a lock that wasn't bent at all, and when he closed it and found that no amount of pulling would make it slip open, he had to admit the truth.

Rex had not escaped. He had been stolen. While Jimmy lay in bed and had silly nightmares, somebody had come and taken Rex away, probably in a truck — the very truck Jimmy had heard!

But who? It couldn't be the man with the whip this time. How could he know they were here? It must have been somebody else, an ordinary thief or a gang of thieves. "I'll just see if they left any tracks," Jimmy thought, "and then I'll wake Charley. He'll know what to do. He'll get Rex back for me!"

The flashlight showed that the stones of the driveway had been scuffed about by many feet, but there was no way of knowing which were old scuffs and which were new. Jimmy knelt to examine one of them more closely, and made a discovery. Among the gray stones he found some brown, light, puffy grains. He picked one up, smelled it, and touched it with his tongue. It was Puffed Wheat!

A little farther along he found some more grains, and then some more. It was a regular trail of Puffed Wheat, and it led all the way to the road where a smear of oil, still fresh and wet, marked the parking place of the mysterious truck. So *that* was the reason Rex had gone so quietly! He would go anywhere, with anyone at all, for Puffed Wheat. Suddenly Jimmy realized what that meant.

Nobody in this town knew that Rex liked the cereal. Aunt Ella didn't use it, and she gave Rex so many other good things that Jimmy had never bothered to buy a box. The Dixons, on the farm, hadn't used it either. In fact, only four people in the world knew about Rex's fondness for that particular breakfast cereal — Jimmy, the Mudges, and the man with the whip!

This changed everything. In all his travels he had never told any grownup why he was running away. Should he do it now? Always, when he had a problem, he had taken it to Rex first, and now he went into the empty garage and sat down on the wooden box he used as a chair. It stood beside the pile of straw which had been Rex's bed.

Charley and Aunt Ella would certainly believe him, and even the man with the whip couldn't out-argue Aunt Ella! Why, if the Mudges told Aunt Ella that Jimmy had stolen Rex, Aunt Ella would say, "Nonsense! He belongs to Jimmy!" and then she might say, "Any fool could see that Jimmy is a fine, honest boy, and you are a villain!" And Charley would agree with her. So what was he waiting for?

He jumped to his feet, but his arm brushed something from the lid of Rex's feed bin. When he turned his flashlight on the floor, he found that it was only a carrot, but something white had fluttered down also — a piece of paper. In the yellowish circle of the flashlight, the words stood out bold and black.

FORGET THE ELEPHANT OR YOU WILL GO TO JAIL FOR STEALING HIM. IF YOUR FINE FRIENDS BUTT IN, THEY'LL BE LOCKED UP FOR HIDING STOLEN PROPERTY.

THIS IS A WARNING!

P.S. PEOPLE WHO TRY TO HIDE SHOULDN'T GET THEIR PICTURES IN THE PAPER.

So that was how they had found him — the picture of Rex at the charity bazaar. This letter changed everything! Charley and Aunt Ella wouldn't pay any attention to threats. They would go right on trying to get Rex back, and end up in all kinds of trouble, maybe even in jail! He couldn't let that happen. They had been too good to him and to Rex!

He must find Rex himself. And he had better leave right away, before they woke up and started asking questions! He let himself into the house again and tiptoed up to his room. The note he left on the pillow said simply:

GOOD-BY. WE HAVE TO GO AWAY. THANK YOU FOR EVERYTHING.

JIMMY AND REX McLEAN

In one pocket he put his money — his gas-station tips, and what was left of his piggy-bank money. In the other he put his baseball cap, his harmonica, and Rex's cap with the red and yellow ribbons. Then, after a last glance at his familiar room, he tiptoed down the stairs again.

Chapter Eighteen. WISKAPOTAMI

WHERE was Rex? Somewhere in a truck, speeding along — and wherever he went, Jimmy must follow and find him. But how? With the whole country to hide him in . . .

For a moment Jimmy almost gave up, and then he began to think. It wasn't as bad as that. A truck had to travel on a highway. If it was going a long way, it would probably take one of the main highways, and turn off later. The only main highway nearby ran north and south, and not too far north was the border. They couldn't take Rex out of the country without a lot of papers and things — so there was a good chance they had taken the highway going south.

If Jimmy followed the highway and inquired at every gas station, he *might* find someone who had seen Rex. After all, the truck had to stop for gas, and the man with the whip had to eat — and an elephant is pretty hard to hide! Even if Jimmy didn't catch up with him right away, he might trail him, and then — well, then he would see!

All day Sunday he tramped along the highway, taking

lifts whenever he could get them, and asking everyone he met, "Have you seen an elephant on a truck?"

A lot of people laughed and gave him silly answers, but he kept on asking anyway. It was hot and dusty, and, for the first time, traveling was no fun. With Rex, everything had been an adventure, but now all he could think of was the man with the whip "whipping Rex into shape."

Jimmy's plan had seemed a good one when he started, but now with every mile it looked more hopeless. Any little side road could be the one the truck had turned on — or had it gone north and then turned? He spent the night in a haystack and woke early, feeling itchy and prickly and unhappy. Brushing himself off as well as he could, he slid under the fence and started along the highway, not even bothering to ask for a lift.

Suddenly a car screeched to a stop beside him and a voice said, "You're out early, boy! Going my way? Hop in!" As Jimmy climbed in and closed the door, the car shot off again.

"Thanks," said Jimmy. "I —" but that was all he got a chance to say. Mr. Wilmott was a brush salesman; he sold forty-seven kinds of brushes — " 'A brush for every job! You've got the job, we've got the brush!' That's our slogan, boy! Now, how about breakfast? Hate to eat alone. Here! This looks like a nice place!"

Jimmy traveled with Mr. Wilmott almost all that day. He was the perfect lift for Jimmy's purpose — he stopped at every small town and roadside store to sell his brushes

and when Jimmy asked to stop at gas stations to ask about his elephant, Mr. Wilmott said, "Why not? You never know who needs a brush! Why, I could tell you stories —" And he did. Some of them were quite interesting, but Jimmy hardly heard him. At last Mr. Wilmott said, "Well, I turn left here at the crossroads. Which way for you, boy?"

Jimmy said, "I think I'll get out here, thanks. I — I haven't made up my mind."

"Suit yourself!" said Mr. Wilmott. "Sorry to lose the company. Hope you find your elephant . . . you never did tell me how you came to lose one. Well, maybe next time! Good luck!"

Left at the crossroads, Jimmy wondered what he should do. Both roads were main highways, and the truck might have turned either way, or gone straight ahead. Well, he would just have to follow one road for a while, and then come back and try another. But first he would ask at the Crossroads Diner, and he might eat there too. Lunch with Mr. Wilmott had been a long time ago.

There were several big transports drawn up in front of the diner, and the girl behind the counter seemed to know all the drivers. She never stopped laughing and joking with them even while she was making Jimmy's wheat-cakes and pouring his milk. He had to interrupt her to ask: "Excuse me, have you seen an elephant around here lately?"

"An *elephant?*" Her voice rose to a surprised screech. "Who you kidding? Last time I saw an elephant was when I was a little kid —" she leaned on the counter and looked sad. "I still remember it!" she said. "My Pop took me to the circus —"

A big truck driver looked up from his pie with two scoops of ice cream. "It just so happens that I saw an elephant this morning," he said. "It wasn't so far from here, either. At first I thought I was seein' things, but —"

"Was he in a truck? Was it a baby elephant? Did he look scared?"

The truck driver scratched his head. "Oh gosh, it was just an elephant. I was driving through this town, and I saw this elephant doing tricks and a lot of children watching. Maybe there was a man collecting money — I'm not sure. But that's all I saw!" He swallowed a large mouthful of strawberry ice cream. Jimmy was almost frantic.

"Do you remember where it was?" he asked.

The driver looked offended. "Sure I do!" he said. "You think I'm a dope or something? It was just this morning, before my last stop. Let's see now. Seaton? Nope. Elbow Bend? No-o-o — I think it was something like Willow."

The girl behind the counter was interested. "Wilmot? Wildwood? Waring?" she suggested.

"Wiskapotami Falls!" said the driver triumphantly. "I saw the elephant at Wiskapotami Falls!"

"I've got to get there right away!" said Jimmy. "Which road do I take? How far is it?" He was already at the door, but the girl called: "Wait! If you're in such a big hurry — Hey! any of you guys going south to Wiskapotami?"

The ride only took an hour and a half, but to Jimmy it felt more like a week before the driver said: "Coming into Wiskapotami now. There's the park over there — near the falls. Looks like something going on, with all those kids — Hey! There's the elephant!"

"Rex!" said Jimmy. Before the truck stopped rolling he jumped out, landed running, and raced across the grass towards the far side of the park. There, dark against the setting sun, a huge shape towered over a crowd of children.

But even while he ran, he knew that something was

wrong. The towering shape was too high, and when he called, "Rex!" it paid no attention.

It wasn't Rex.

It was a strange elephant.

Chapter Nineteen.   A NEW LEAD

AT FIRST Jimmy refused to believe it. After all his searching, he *couldn't* have found the wrong elephant! But there it was — there *she* was — sitting on a silly little chair and holding aloft another chair on which her trainer sat, calmly smoking a cigarette.

She was much bigger than Rex, and Jimmy thought she looked old and sad, with her wrinkled skin that hung loose like a too-large suit of clothes and her legs criss-crossed with old scars. Her trainer looked as old and sorry-looking as she, with his stained clothes and battered hat and stubble of gray whiskers, but Jimmy could see that he was no man with a whip. As the elephant finished each trick he patted her trunk and said, "Good girl, Molly!" and once, when he wasn't looking, the trunk sneaked into his trouser pocket and came out with a carrot. All the children laughed and the trainer pretended to be very angry, but Molly didn't seem at all frightened. In fact, she waved the carrot in front of his face before she popped it into her mouth!

The sun was almost gone now, and several mothers

had come and were urging their children to leave, but the children didn't want to go. When the old man saw this he bowed, and as he did so Molly lifted the hat from his head and carried it around the circle of children and mothers. A few dropped coins into it, and one put in an apple. Molly's owner gave her the apple, slipped the small handful of money into his pocket, and said, "Thanks a lot, folks! Show's over!"

A few people waited to make sure it really was over, but at last they drifted away too, and only Jimmy was left. The old man was sitting on the ground now. He had spread out a not-too-clean handkerchief, and was counting his money on it. Most of the coins were nickels and pennies. When he looked up and saw Jimmy standing beside his elephant, he said, "Run along, Sonny. Show's over!"

"I just wanted to look at her." Jimmy was patting the elephant now, and her restless trunk was gently feeling his pockets. "Sorry!" he told her. "No carrots. I haven't even got an apple for you."

"Run along!" said the old man crossly. "If you don't, I'll tell Molly to sit on you!"

Jimmy put his arm around Molly's trunk the way he had seen the old man do a little while earlier. "Up, Molly!" he said, and she obeyed immediately. When the trainer saw Jimmy sitting on his elephant's head and scratching gently behind her ear with the toe of his shoe he was really surprised.

"Come down off that!" he said. "Molly, what's the idea? Now, young man —"

Still scratching behind Molly's ear, Jimmy explained about Rex — how he had lost him and been sure that the elephant at Wiskapotami must be his pet. He even showed the two baseball caps and the warning note.

The old man seemed excited and angry too. "The man who wrote that note!" he said. "What does he look like? Does he always carry a whip?"

"That's right!" Jimmy said. "He has black, shiny hair, and he keeps tapping that whip against his boot all the time. He isn't a friend of yours, is he?"

"A friend of *mine?* Sylvester Sykes, the worst — oh, Molly girl, I'm sorry!"

At the sound of the name, the old elephant had reared up, flinging her trunk high and trumpeting in terror. Jimmy had never seen an elephant so frightened. He managed to hold on while the old man petted and soothed her, and then ordered her to kneel so Jimmy could slide off. Then, feeding her carrots and speaking in a soothing tone, the old man said softly, "Poor Molly knows *him*, too well. She's one elephant they took away from him in time to save her life, but she's a broken-down old lady when she should still be in her prime. I had to stop carrying a whip, even though I never used it, and she can't stand noise or big crowds —"

"Rex!" said Jimmy. "I have to rescue him! But — I don't know where to look!"

The old man eyed him kindly. "Have you tried the State Fair?" he asked. "If I had a healthy young elephant right now, and wanted to make some money —"

"Where?" asked Jimmy. "How do I get there? You'll come with me, won't you?"

The old man shook his head. "Old Molly could never stand the crowds," he said. "We're working our way south now, before the cold weather. You're going to need help, though. You can't just walk up and say, 'Give me my elephant!'"

"The Mudges would come," agreed Jimmy. "They would say Rex wasn't mine at all. But if you'll just tell me where it is, I'll think of *something*. I've *got* to!"

The old man was thinking. "Just a minute," he said. "Molly, girl, who do we know — of course! Jimmy, you go to the fair. Find one of the performers in the Big Top show, and ask for Frightened Fred. He'll help you if he can. He hates you-know-who as much as we do. He knew Molly in the old days."

"Who is he?" asked Jimmy. "And if he's frightened, how can he help? What's he scared of?"

The old man seemed very pleased with himself. "Oh, practically everything frightens Fred, but don't let that bother you! Just tell him that old Dan and Molly sent you!"

Chapter Twenty.   FRIGHTENED FRED

I T WAS late Friday afternoon when Jimmy rode into the fairgrounds on a truck with six black-faced sheep.

Old Dan had told him, "Go to the Big Top — the circus tent on the Midway." So, after helping the farmer to unload his sheep, Jimmy hurried from the Animal Exhibits building. He passed the exhibits of grain and canned goods and farm implements, and was soon on the booth-lined street of the Midway.

Overhead, the little seats on the Ferris wheel tilted and rose in orderly procession, and riders on the roller-coaster screamed as they plunged down the big dip, but Jimmy had no time to watch them now. He dodged between strolling families, and pushed through the gaping crowd in front of a tent marked SEVEN WONDERS OF THE WORLD. "Hur-ry, hur-ry, hur-ry —" a man was droning into a microphone. "*Tell* you what I'm gonna do —" but Jimmy didn't stop to hear him. At the end of the street, just beyond the Seven Wonders, stood an enormous gray tent trimmed with colored pennants — the Big Top.

Jimmy wondered how he could find someone called

Frightened Fred in all the crowd of a circus. Perhaps, if he asked at the ticket booth . . .

But the ticket booth was closed and there was no crowd. The big tent seemed deserted. A rope was stretched across to bar the wide entrance, but there was nobody to stop him from ducking under the rope and going in.

The emptiness made the place look even bigger, and it was bigger than the Civic Stadium back home. At the far end, on a raised bandstand, wooden chairs were ranged in rows. The sawdust ring was surrounded by tiers of benches, all empty. Overhead dangled empty trapezes.

"You're late for the afternoon show, boy, and three hours too early for the next one!"

Jimmy jumped. He hadn't noticed the man with the trumpet, but there he sat, on a wooden box. The sleeves of his red-and-gold uniform were turned up, and he was polishing his horn with a dirty cloth. When Jimmy explained that he was looking for Frightened Fred, the man laid down his cloth and horn and came to the door.

"See those trailers back there?" he said. "The green one in the third row — that's Fred's. But if it's an autograph you want, I'll give you mine."

As he knocked at the trailer door, Jimmy wondered what he should call the man who answered. Frightened Fred wasn't a very *nice* nickname. It might be better to say, "I'm looking for *Mr.* Fred."

"No use knocking on my door," said a voice behind him. "I'm not home."

Jimmy whirled around — then he laughed. "You're Frightened Fred!" he said.

Frightened Fred was a clown. His lips were a painted red O in the middle of his chalk-white face, his eyebrows were red V's on his high forehead, and his hair, which seemed to be green, stood straight up in bristles!

"Were you looking for me?" asked the clown.

"If you are Frightened Fred."

"Scare me!" said the clown. "Say 'Boo!'"

"Boo!" said Jimmy.

Springing into the air, the clown turned a back somersault, his big clown shoes running frantically all the time.

He landed on his feet, bowed, and said, "Frightened Fred, at your service. What can I do for you?"

"Ðan and Old Molly sent me," Jimmy told him. "Dan said you would help me find my elephant."

Frightened Fred scratched his green bristles. "Come into my trailer," he said at last. "I'm afraid you won't find your elephant there, but you can tell me about it while I get out of my makeup." He unlocked the door, and Jimmy followed him in. "Now!" said Fred. "Sit down on that bunk. Begin at the beginning, go on to the end, and then stop!"

Obediently, Jimmy settled himself cross-legged on the bunk. "I got this elephant for my birthday," he began. "His name was Rex . . ."

He told the whole story, and while he talked Fred stepped out of the baggy clown suit and big shoes and lifted off the green wig. (His own hair was black with a bald spot in the middle.) Then he sat down at a battered wooden dressing table and spread cold cream on his face to take off the paint. By the time Jimmy had finished, Frightened Fred the clown was gone. In his place sat a thin man in trousers and undershirt who slapped his knee and said, "So that's where Sykes got the elephant!"

"Rex is here?" Jimmy jumped up. "Where can I find him? Is he all right? You'll help me get him back, won't you?"

"You'd better sit down again," said Frightened Fred.

"He's all right, isn't he? That Sykes man hasn't —"

"Rex is fine," said Frightened Fred reassuringly. "Sykes has been a perfect little gent — so far. But where do you think you're going?"

"To see Rex, of course. To get him back!"

"I suppose you're going to walk up to Sykes and say, 'Give me back my elephant'?"

Jimmy sank down on the edge of the bunk again. "He wouldn't give Rex back," he said miserably. "He'd — I don't know what he'd do. But I thought, if you would help —"

"He'd send for those Mudge people and they'd take you away. How could I help you then? And if you tried to get away with Rex, you'd never get off the grounds. I don't know how we could — Wait! When did you say your father would be back?"

"The first of September," said Jimmy.

"Hmmm," Fred rubbed his chin. "Another ten days. But the fair will be here for two weeks — it just started yesterday. I think the best thing you can do —"

Jimmy leaned forward. "What?" he asked.

"Let Sykes keep Rex," said Frightened Fred.

Sadly, Jimmy rose. "I guess I'd better be going," he said. "I'm sorry you can't help me, but I'll just have to figure some way —"

Frightened Fred laughed. "Sit down!" he said. "Sit down and listen! If Sykes doesn't know you're on his trail, he'll stay right here. If he stays here, we can keep an eye on him until we can get in touch with your father.

If we scare him and he takes Rex away now, who knows where he'll go? Understand?"

"I — think so." Jimmy hesitated. "But how about Rex? What will Sykes do to him in ten days?"

"I think Rex will be all right," said Fred. "I happen to know that Sykes had a hard time getting this job, with his reputation and a half-trained young elephant. If he makes good here, he may get a contract somewhere for the winter. That's what he wants. There are scouts from other outfits looking us over all the time. They know we break up soon.

"So Sykes is on his best behavior. With us on the spot to watch him, I think Rex should be all right!"

Jimmy took a deep breath. He felt as though he hadn't been breathing properly for a long time. "You said *we* can watch him," he said happily. "That means you'll let me hide here, doesn't it? I promise to stay out of sight!"

Fred shook his head. "No good!" he said. "Within twenty-four hours everyone on the lot would know that I was hiding someone, and most of them would know his name. No, Jimmy McLean must go!"

"I won't leave Rex again!" said Jimmy. "I —"

Fred laughed. "Simmer down!" he said. "I told you Jimmy McLean couldn't stay, and I meant it. If *you* want to stay, you'll just have to be somebody else. Now, how would you like to be my cousin, name of Buddy? And I said you can't *hide* here, and you can't. Have you ever thought of joining a circus?"

"I'll do anything!" said Jimmy. "I'll wash dishes, or carry water to the animals, or —"

"You stay away from the animals!" ordered Fred. "Do you want Rex to recognize you and give us away? I mean *really* join the show. I could use an assistant in my act. If you're interested —"

"You mean — I could be a *clown?*" Jimmy couldn't quite believe it.

Fred smiled. "It's a pretty good idea, don't you think so? Who would ever guess that you were hiding, out there in front of the whole audience?"

"But Mr. Sykes will know me!"

"Not after I get through with you," said Fred. "Let's see, now — we'll start with your hair." He poured something from a bottle into a basin of water, and washed Jimmy's hair twice with it. Then he poured a little of the solution into a saucer, and carefully touched up his eyebrows with a toothbrush dipped in a saucer. Then he combed Jimmy's hair, stood back, and whistled. "That's almost enough," he said. "Just one more thing —" He put something from his makeup kit on two of Jimmy's front teeth, and handed him a mirror. "Meet my Cousin Buddy!" he said.

Jimmy glanced in the mirror — and then he stared! A strange boy stared back at him. Jimmy had always worn his dark hair parted at the side, but Cousin Buddy had blond hair slicked straight back. Jimmy had black eyebrows, Buddy's were blond — such a light blond that they made his tanned skin look several shades darker. And two of his front teeth seemed to be missing! He was just running his tongue along them to make sure they were still there, when Fred said, "You can stop admiring yourself, Buddy. Didn't you hear the dinner bell? We'll have to do some tall hustling if we're going to work up some sort of costume and act for you in time for the eight o'clock show — and we'd better be good, if we want the ringmaster to let you stay. Besides, I'm hungry. Come on!"

Chapter Twenty-One. THE FIFTH CLOWN

MY *name is Buddy. My name is Buddy,* Jimmy reminded himself as he and Fred approached the mess tent. I've come to work with my cousin Fred. I mustn't stare as though I'd never seen circus people before. . . .

But as they made their way between the long tables towards two vacant places, Jimmy felt a little disappointed; there seemed to be nothing to stare at. He wasn't sure just what he had expected — bright costumes, perhaps; tights, and spangles, and people hanging upside down from trapezes. They couldn't *eat* upside down, he told himself scornfully. And drinking would be even worse. . . . What he had *not* expected was rows of ordinary-looking people in summer clothes, eating and chatting. And such ordinary chatter! As he and Fred sat down, a motherly voice farther down the table was saying, "If you don't eat those vegetables, Sydney, there'll be no pie for you. And this time I'm not fooling!"

All Jimmy could see of the speaker was a broad back in

a printed dress, and the back of a dark head bristling with metal curlers. But when Fred said, "Kate! I want you to meet my cousin, Buddy!" she turned around and Jimmy nearly dropped the fork he had just picked up. Her plump chin was framed in metal curlers too — curlers full of dark hair!

"Kate Kincaid is our bearded lady."

"As if he couldn't see that!" laughed Kate. "Glad to know you, Buddy. I want you to meet my little boy. . . . Sydney! What are you doing?" Caught in the act of dumping his carrots and peas under the table, the five-year-old Sydney was led howling from the tent.

When his first appetite was satisfied, Jimmy began to look around. He realized now that this might not be such an ordinary crowd — ordinary crowds did not include bearded ladies! A booming laugh drew his attention to the back of the tent. The man who laughed was so big that, even sitting down, his head nearly brushed the canvas roof. But his table companions were tiny — at first Jimmy thought they were children, and then he realized that one of the "children" was almost bald. They must be midgets!

The almost-bald midget seemed to be telling funny stories. Suddenly the giant burst into guffaws of laughter, and this time he laughed so hard that he choked and started to cough. The lady midget sitting beside him tried to pat his back, but she couldn't reach high enough, even when she stood on the bench. A man from the next table had to come over. He was of ordinary size, but his bald head was completely covered with tattooing!

This really was a circus! Bearded lady, tattooed man, giant, midgets — what other interesting people would there be? Twisting around to get a better view of the tent, Jimmy found himself face to face with Mr. Sykes, the man with the whip.

For an awful moment Jimmy's mind screamed *Run!* — while his body refused to move a muscle. Then he realized that Sykes, after looking straight at him, was scowling at his pie again. Jimmy's disguise must be all right — so far, anyway.

"What's the matter, Buddy? Don't you like the stew?" asked Fred. Jimmy picked up his fork. The first few mouthfuls almost choked him, but when Sykes stalked out of the tent, whip in hand, his appetite returned. He finished his stew, polished off the last of the gravy with a bit of bread, and when the girl brought hot peach pie, he held out his milk glass for her to refill.

Then — "Finished?" said Fred. "Good. Let's go. I've been thinking about your costume. If you were a little taller or a little fatter, we might make one of mine do. . . . Fatter . . . Now, there's an idea!"

The circus program said FOUR WONDERFUL CLOWNS but that night the audience saw five. The first three were billed as THE JUGGLING JOKERS, and they threw things at each other until the air was full of flying plates and hoops and hats. The act ended with all the hats piled on the head of one clown, and all the hoops around the neck of the second, while the third held a plate in each hand and balanced a third on the end of his nose!

The fourth clown was called Frightened Fred. He had bristling green hair, and as he stood in the doorway looking at the audience, another clown came up behind him and frightened him by blowing a whistle. Frightened Fred jumped into the air and turned a somersault, his clown shoes running all the time.

The clown who frightened Fred wasn't on the program at all. He was short and fat — about as tall as a twelve-year-old boy, and as fat as a boy might be with pillows under his clown suit, fore and aft. He had a big blue putty nose, and he wore a white nightcap with a red tassel. The laughter of the crowd seemed to frighten the fat clown. He looked up suddenly, tripped over his long clown shoes, and fell over on his back. The crowd thought that was very funny, but when he tried to get up and couldn't, and lay there kicking and struggling like an overturned turtle, the audience roared. As Fred pulled him up, he whispered, "We'll keep that in the act. Come on. Have you got your water pistol?"

Jimmy frightened Fred twice more that night. Once he held him up with the water pistol, and once Fred lay on the ground pretending to be asleep and Jimmy tiptoed up and blew an enormous horn in his ear. The horn let out

a silly little squeak, and again Fred turned a back somersault.

Between their acts, Jimmy and Fred watched the rest
of the show from the bottom step of the bandstand. The
pony act was very good, and there was a man who did
stunts on a bicycle that kept falling apart. Once Fred was
frightened by a trained seal, and once the smallest of the
performing dogs jumped out of its trainer's pocket and
chased Fred all the way around the ring. Jimmy had almost
forgotten why he was here — he was still laughing at
Fred and the dog — when the next act came through the
entrance. The next act was Rex, with the man with the
whip!

Mr. Sykes wore white riding breeches now, and his
shiny boots were as black and slick as his patent-leather
hair. He smiled and bowed to the audience and patted Rex
as though he loved him, but he still carried the same short,
ugly whip. Poor Rex looked unhappy. The mischief was
gone from his eye, and he did his tricks with a sort of
nervous speed, watching the whip all the time.

From his place on the bottom step of the bandstand,
Jimmy watched every move in the ring. All went well
until Rex tried to balance a small chair on the end of his
trunk. This was a new trick — Sykes must have taught it
to him — and Rex had trouble with it. After juggling the
chair for a few seconds, he dropped it, and Sykes, still
smiling at the audience, gave Rex a short, vicious cut with
the whip.

The audience could not see what he had done, but Jimmy saw and jumped to his feet. If Fred hadn't seized the back of his clown suit, he would have given himself away then and there. But Fred hung on, and the audience laughed to see the fat clown running and running without getting anywhere.

"Blow your horn!" commanded Fred. "Frighten me!" Jimmy seized the horn and blew it in Fred's face, Fred tugged the back of his suit so hard that he fell over, and then Fred tumbled down on top of him. By the time they were both on their feet again, the elephant act was over and Rex and Mr. Sykes were gone.

Jimmy hardly noticed the rest of the show, not even the lion act when the ringmaster stood outside the cage with a gun in his hand in case of trouble. Jimmy was thinking of Rex, his pet and his friend, in the hands of a villain like Sykes. How could he do nothing for ten whole days and let Sykes treat Rex like that? He would *have* to do something!

On their way out, the ringmaster met them. "It's all right, Fred," he said. "You can keep the young man in your act." He turned to Jimmy. "Glad to have you with us, Buddy!" he said kindly.

"So *that's* all right," said Fred. "Nothing to worry about now!" But just outside the performers' entrance they found Mr. Sykes waiting for them — an angry Mr. Sykes. Had he recognized Jimmy?

Sykes strode right past him and shook his whip under

Fred's nose. "You!" he said. "What do you mean by clowning while my act is on? You try to take the audience away from me again, and I'll —"

"You'll do what?" asked Fred coolly. "Complain to the management? Tell them that you can't hold your own audience? Let me tell *you* that any time you mistreat that elephant — in the ring or out of it — I'll *really* steal your audience. A fat chance you'll have of getting a winter contract, then. And if you shake that whip at me again, I'll break it in half! Come on, Buddy!"

He stalked off, and Jimmy trotted behind, trying to thank him. Fred didn't give him a chance. "Look!" he said. "I've got an idea for another routine! I'm asleep, see, with my head on a balloon. You come tiptoeing up with a long pin. I've got some balloons in the trailer. Come on, let's try it right away!"

Chapter Twenty-Two. ANNE-MARIE

Jimmy and Fred were up early the next morning practicing the balloon-and-pin routine. After breakfast Fred worked on Jimmy's costume, sewing the places they had only pinned the night before. There was nothing Jimmy could do to help, so Fred said, "Why don't you go out and have a look around? If you're back by eleven, we'll have time to run through the act once more before lunch."

It was a fine, bright morning. As Jimmy strolled along, his hands in his pockets, he wondered why the Midway seemed different today. People still screamed on the rushing roller-coaster, the merry-go-round horses still rose and fell to their tinny, exciting music, and people still walked along eating pickles and ice cream and hot dogs and candy floss and potato chips. He sniffed the air, and decided that the smells were the same, yet something had changed. Suddenly he realized what it was. It's me! thought Jimmy. I feel different today!

Wherever he looked he saw boys and girls with money to spend on rides, and food, and games. His pockets were empty, but instead of feeling jealous he was almost sorry for them. This afternoon, they would be lining up to spend their money on circus tickets, paying to see him and the other clowns and circus acts. And after the show, they would have to go home. They were just audience. He was a part of all this!

He stopped to watch a fat woman trying to win a stuffed elephant at the Wheel of Fortune. At the other end of the counter, a small girl in blouse and shorts was watching. Jimmy didn't want her to think he was just another customer, so when the fat lady left (she had won a comb, an ash tray, and a pencil that wrote red at one end and blue at the other, but no elephant) he spoke to the man behind the counter.

"Good day for business!" he said. "I hope this nice weather keeps up!"

The man stared at him. "You wanna play?" he said. "Let's see your dime!"

"I don't have one right now —" said Jimmy. "I only—"

"Beat it, then, and come back when you have one!" said the man. "You kids hang around all day and don't leave any room for customers!"

Jimmy moved away, trying to look as though it were his own idea. The little girl trailed after him. She was quite small — her head was no higher than his shoulder — and Jimmy thought, I'll bet she never talked to a real clown! Aloud he said, "That fellow didn't have to be so nasty. I was just being polite. Show people should stick together!"

She looked at him with wide brown eyes. "You are show people?" She had a slight foreign accent.

"Yes," said Jimmy kindly. "I'm with the circus myself. I'm a clown."

"A *clown?*"

"That's right," said Jimmy. "We have a very good show. You shouldn't miss it. You see, we —"

The small girl giggled.

Jimmy was surprised. He didn't think he had said anything funny. But before he could say anything, the wail of a child in distress made them both stop and turn around.

The wail became a howl. A gas-filled balloon had escaped from its young owner's hand and sailed off over the low booths. Now it was stopped temporarily, because its string had caught on a nail in the roof of the two-story House of Fun, but the tugging breeze threatened to release it at any moment.

A ladder! thought Jimmy. "If only —"

"Stop her, somebody!" a woman screamed.

"Good girl, Anne-Marie! You'll get your balloon back, Sonny!" said the man in the fish-pond booth. The little boy was gaping upwards, the tears still making tracks down his dusty cheeks, and more and more people were turning and pointing and staring.

The cause of the commotion was Jimmy's small companion. In the time it took him to think of a ladder, she had darted forward, tugged at a rope hanging down the side of the Fun House, and now she was halfway up, climbing like a monkey. Reaching the top, she ran lightly across the roof and retrieved the balloon, then started down with the string between her teeth. When she saw the crowd looking up at her, she stopped and seemed to fall backwards. The crowd gasped, and a woman screamed; then they saw that she had twined the rope around one leg. For a moment she dangled upside-down before she straightened up, slid down the rope, and returned the balloon to its owner. Paying no attention to the applauding crowd, she walked away sedately at Jimmy's side.

"You were telling me about circuses," she said when they had reached a quiet place between two tents. Jimmy hadn't said anything. He couldn't think of anything to say! "It must be wonderful to belong to a circus —" said the little girl, bending backwards until she looked up at him between her legs. "It must be . . . Your face! You should see your face!" She collapsed on the grass, helpless with laughter.

Jimmy didn't know what to do. It was silly to stand here and be laughed at — people were stopping to stare — but if he walked away and left her rolling on the ground he would feel even sillier. She was a very rude little girl.

Suddenly he realized just how funny it was. He must have looked very silly, telling her about the circus, when all the time she was a real acrobat. The more he thought about it, the funnier it seemed. He began to laugh too, and then he couldn't stop! The girl was just beginning

to recover, but this set her off again. As they sat on the ground at last, weak with laughter, the child they had called Anne-Marie wiped her eyes.

"I'm sorry!" she said. "I guess I shouldn't have laughed at you."

"I'm a clown, aren't I?" said Jimmy. "I'm supposed to make people laugh!"

Suddenly, they were friends. As they got up and brushed themselves off, Anne-Marie said, "You must be Frightened Fred's new assistant. Your name is Buddy, isn't it?"

Jimmy had almost forgotten that his name was Buddy. "That's right!" he said.

"I'm Anne-Marie Dumont," she told him. "You saw my parents last night. THE FLYING DUMONTS, FRANCE'S TRAPEZE ARTISTES EXTRAORDINARY — that's what the program calls them."

"You're French?" said Jimmy. "But you speak English —"

"We have been here, it is four years!" said Anne-Marie. "My English is all right, but you should hear my German. I was so small when we were in Germany. And I have no Spanish at all. Have you Spanish?"

"No," said Jimmy. "I have only — I mean, I speak only English. How old are you? Are you part of the show? I didn't see you last night."

Anne-Marie turned two cartwheels. When she was right side up again, she said, "I will soon be twelve. I am not yet in the show, but perhaps soon, if I practice hard" — she stopped, picked up one foot, and put it behind her neck. They were just passing the merry-go-round.

"Anne-Marie!" called the merry-go-round man. "It's eleven o'clock! Your Dad said if I saw you, I should tell you the time!"

"Oh my goodness!" said Anne-Marie. "Late for practice! And Papa hates to be kept waiting! I will see you, Buddy!" Three cartwheels carried her into the thick of the crowd and she was gone.

Chapter Twenty-Three. BANANA CAKE
AND A
MAIL-ORDER FLUTE

O N SUNDAY, as they sat down to breakfast, Fred said: "No show today. Have you made any plans yet?"

"Not yet," said Jimmy, spreading jam on his toast. "I'll have to think about it."

He didn't have much time to think. When he and Fred left the tent, they found Anne-Marie waiting for them. She was hopping with impatience, and began to speak as soon as she saw them.

"Mama said I must not disturb your breakfast but I thought you would never stop eating!" she said. "Fred — I am to ask you if Buddy can spend the day with us. Mama thought you might need him for practice but you can practice after supper, can't you?"

"Well —" said Fred, "I guess —"

"Oh, thank you, Fred! Buddy, we leave for church in fifteen minutes. I'll meet you in front of my place but now I must run and get dressed because Papa hates to be kept waiting!"

She was gone before Jimmy could open his mouth, and he must have looked surprised because Fred laughed and said, "It's a good thing you didn't make any plans!"

When he got to the Dumont trailer, Anne-Marie's father was sitting in the car, and Mrs. Dumont was on the trailer steps tying Anne-Marie's hair with a pink bow. Mrs. Dumont wore a big white apron and looked exactly like a mother, and not like a trapeze artist at all. When she spoke, she sounded like a mother, too.

"Buddy!" she said. "You will keep an eye on Anne-Marie? Do not let her forget she must be a lady, not an acrobat, until she comes home and changes her clothes!"

"Mama!" said Anne-Marie, sitting down carefully and smoothing out her fluffy skirt. "How *could* I forget? This is my new dress — oh, Buddy, can you walk on your hands? When we get out of the car, I will show you a trick —"

Mr. Dumont started the engine. "We will go now!" he said. "Otherwise, Anne-Marie will be walking to church on her hands! Good-by, Mama, we — is something burning?"

"The cake!" Mrs. Dumont disappeared into the trailer.

"Mama goes to church in the evening," Anne-Marie explained as they drove away. "All day Sunday, she cooks and cooks."

"Next to her family and trapeze, she loves her stove best!" said Anne-Marie's father. "Sometimes I think the stove comes first, and I would be jealous — if I did not enjoy so much eating what she cooks!"

Jimmy saw what he meant when they got back from church. One end of the Dumont trailer was furnished as a kitchen with a small stove and refrigerator, a glass-fronted cabinet displaying gay dishes, and a table which folded against the wall. But now the table, the stove, and even the top of the cabinet were crowded with good things to eat, each more delicious than the last. When they came at last to a tremendous banana cake, Jimmy regretfully shook his head.

"But you must!" said Mrs. Dumont. "How can I make lemon pie for supper with all this cake left over? It must not be wasted! Just a tiny piece, Buddy?"

Jimmy eyed the cake, then drew a deep breath. "I wish I had room!" he said.

"I know!" said Mrs. Dumont. "I will give you a piece for Frightened Fred, and one for you, later, when you have room. And you and Anne-Marie can take pieces this afternoon to Uncle James and Mr. Finlay and the Pierces."

Already she was cutting and wrapping generous portions of the cake. Anne-Marie had vanished behind a curtain which divided the trailer into two rooms, and before her mother had finished she was back, dressed in her old shorts and blouse and walking on her hands. She still wore the pink hair bow.

"Buddy will carry the basket!" said Mrs. Dumont. "Up-side-down cake is good, but not upside down on the ground!"

"I could balance it on my feet!" said Anne-Marie.

Mr. Dumont laughed. "I tried that once," he said. "It was a basket of dishes. Your mother still remembers!"

"Give our love to Uncle James and tell him to come in for lemon pie after church tonight," said Mrs. Dumont. "And don't eat too much this afternoon — I don't want you to spoil your supper!"

Mr. Finlay's trailer was the biggest in the grounds. Jimmy had noticed it before, and wondered who lived there. It was as high as a big transport trailer, and, like the transports, it rode on big double wheels.

"Anne-Marie! Come in!" Expecting to see a face, Jimmy found himself looking up into a shiny belt buckle. He craned his neck and shifted his gaze higher to meet the beaming blue eyes of Mr. Finlay, the giant.

"Come in!" repeated Mr. Finlay. "You're Buddy, Fred's new assistant? Take my armchair, both of you. That's right — climb up! Sit back and be comfortable. You're not crowded?"

Even if Frightened Fred had been sitting between them, they would not have been crowded in the enormous chair. When they sat back, their legs stuck straight out in front of them, and Jimmy's heels just projected over the edge of the seat.

"I like a nice, roomy chair," said Mr. Finlay happily. "I'm a big man, you know — seven foot six — and I like my comfort!"

He straddled a three-legged stool by the high table and picked up a flute between two fingers like pink bananas. "Lesson Seven came yesterday," he told Anne-Marie. "I got a new piece. I was just practicing before you came in. Would you like to hear me play it?"

"Oh, yes!" said Anne-Marie. She turned to Jimmy. "Mr. Finlay is taking lessons by mail," she told him. "He's very clever!"

The flute looked like a toothpick when Mr. Finlay held it, but the notes he piped so painstakingly sounded quite familiar. Before he had done, Jimmy recognized "There's a Long, Long Trail A-Winding," and Mr. Finlay was delighted. When he heard that Jimmy could play the same tune on his harmonica, he said "We must try a duet very soon! Not today — I don't have that bit in the middle quite clear yet — I'll try it again now."

They struggled out of the big chair and left him tootling happily, while they went on to deliver the next piece of cake.

"The next three pieces!" said Anne-Marie. "There are three people in the Pierce family — Mr. and Mrs. Pierce are the midgets, you know."

"Who's the third midget?" asked Jimmy. "I saw three in the mess tent."

Anne-Marie laughed. "Oh, Edna isn't a midget! She's

their little girl. She's only five years old, and already she's as tall as her mother. Good afternoon, Mrs. Pierce. Mother sent some cake."

"That was very sweet of her. I'm sorry I can't invite you children in." It seemed funny to be called children by someone a head and a half shorter than you were. "But Edna has *spots* today, and I'm keeping her in bed."

"That's too bad!" said Anne-Marie. "I hope she feels better soon."

"Oh, she will. Mr. Pierce is afraid it's measles, but I think it's just too much ice cream. That little Kincaid boy found a dollar yesterday, and the two of them —" she whirled around. "Edna Pierce! Get back in that bed or I'll wallop you, spots or no spots!"

There was only one piece of cake left now, and Jimmy saw that it was a big one. "I saved that for Uncle James," said Anne-Marie. "He's my godfather. He was in France the summer I was born, and he's a regular storybook. Wait till you see!"

Jimmy thought, I suppose she means "Wait till you *hear*." But when the trailer door was opened he saw that Anne-Marie had used the right word after all — though perhaps she should have said "picture book" instead of "storybook." Uncle James was the tattooed man.

When they came in, he was trying to see the top of his bald head in a small mirror and not succeeding very well. "Be with you in a minute," he said. "I can't quite — Anne-Marie, will you look?"

"Look for what, Uncle James?"

"Sunburn," said the tattooed man. "I went out without my cap yesterday. Thought it was cloudy enough. Now my head feels hot!"

Anne-Marie examined his head carefully. "It's a *little* red," she said at last. "The pictures are all quite clear, though."

"If only it doesn't peel!" said Uncle James. "I'll put some lotion on it. Now! This young man is . . . ?"

"Buddy," said Anne-Marie. "He helps Frightened Fred. Mother sent some cake, Uncle James, and I thought if you had time, you would tell us about the snake."

"The snake on my left leg?" Uncle James looked pleased. "Wait! I'll get into my working clothes."

He ducked behind a curtain, and came back a moment later in his "working clothes" — bathing trunks and sandals. Jimmy stared. Every inch of skin seemed to be covered with tattooing.

"Five hundred and twenty-three pictures!" said Uncle James. "A story for every one, too. The snake, now —" The snake wound twice around his left leg, with its head on his kneecap and its tail wrapped around his ankle. "A real snake was the model for this picture," said Uncle James. "It belonged to an old snake-charmer friend of mine."

"Which was your *first* tattoo?" Jimmy asked.

"This little blue anchor on my left wrist," said Uncle James. "Not much story there. I was a sailor lad, you see, about seventeen years old. I was walking down a street in Singapore with my pay in my pocket — after that, one tattoo seemed to lead to another. Anne-Marie? What story will you have next?"

Anne-Marie picked the schooner *Sally Ann* on his left bicep. Uncle James had traveled on that ship, and when he told about the storm at sea, he flexed his muscle and the ship rolled. It was very exciting. It was Jimmy's turn next, and he was just about to ask about the mermaid on Uncle James's chest when the bell rang for supper. He never did find out about that mermaid.

Chapter Twenty-Four. "TICKETS, PLEASE!"

Monday, Tuesday, Wednesday — the days were full. Afternoons and evenings were devoted to the show, and every morning Jimmy and Anne-Marie visited the Midway.

They met after breakfast at the Seven Wonders of the World tent. Usually Jimmy got there first, because Anne-Marie had to help her mother. While he waited, he would visit with Uncle James the tattooed man, and Mr. Finlay the giant, who were two of the Wonders.

It was a good hour for visiting. There were few customers so early in the morning. Mrs. Pierce and Mrs. Kincaid (her beard no longer in curlers) would be knitting and talking about their children, while Mr. Pierce did the morning crossword puzzle and smoked big cigars. The other two Wonders kept pretty much to themselves: the Indian gentleman in the loincloth lay on his bed of spikes and gazed at the roof, and the Strong Man, who was studying to be a dentist, put down his book only when customers came in. Every time he heard the "Hur-ry, hur-ry, hur-ry, step this way, Ladies and Gentlemen!" he would stand up, slip his horn-rimmed glasses into a pocket in his leopardskin, and start bending pokers and straightening horseshoes with his bare hands.

The customers were sometimes very funny. Some were sure that the Pierces were dressed-up children, in spite of Mr. Pierce's bald head and big cigar; some thought that Mrs. Kincaid's beard wasn't real, and once a boy shot a water-pistol at Uncle James to see if the tattooing would wash off!

As soon as Anne-Marie came, they would go out on the Midway. Anne-Marie knew most of the men who ran the rides, so she and Jimmy often rode free on the merry-go-round and the flying boats, and they liked to race in the little cars with the big bumpers (Jimmy usually won).

Thursday morning started as usual. They decided to begin with the merry-go-round, but that was as far as they got.

They found their friend the merry-go-round man trying to run the machine, sell tickets, and collect tickets, all at the same time — his helper hadn't showed up.

"If we could help — " began Anne-Marie.

"You're hired!" said the merry-go-round man. "Now, who does what?"

They decided that Anne-Marie would sell the tickets and that Jimmy would collect them.

"I never sold anything before," said Anne-Marie. "I would like to try, though!"

"It's easy!" Jimmy told her. "You'll do all right!"

And she did, though once or twice she had to ask him for help. As he swung past on the merry-go-round she would call, "Buddy! How much is six children's and two grownups' and change for five dollars?" And the next time he passed, Jimmy would call back, "Six children, ninety cents; two grownups, fifty. Three-sixty change!" The merry-go-round man nodded approval from his place at the operating lever, and Jimmy, grateful for his gas-station training, moved on from horse to horse saying, "Tickets, please!"

Sometimes a small girl clung to the pole with both hands, and he had to pry the ticket carefully from between her fingers. Little children had to be lifted up and helped down, and small boys prevented from jumping off while the machine was still moving fast. And once he told a big boy — at least fifteen years old — "I'm sorry, you'll have to get on a horse. See that sign? Passengers are not allowed to stand on the platform!"

Jimmy wondered what he should do if the helper didn't come at all. He didn't want to leave the merry-go-round man without help, but there was the afternoon show to think of, and Anne-Marie had a Spanish lesson at half-past eleven. Luckily, the fellow came slouching up a little after eleven with a story about someone forgetting to wake him.

"If you didn't play cards all night, you'd be able to get up in the morning!" said the merry-go-round man. "Did Sykes win all your money again?"

"Anne-Marie, come on!" said Jimmy. "It's nearly half-past eleven!" It made him uncomfortable to be so near a friend of Sykes's.

The next morning right after breakfast he went to the merry-go-round, but the helper was there, leaning against a post, with a cigarette dangling from his lower lip. Jimmy waved to the merry-go-round man and went on to the Seven Wonders tent to meet Anne-Marie.

As he approached the tent, he heard the sound of Mr. Finlay's flute. Too bad I didn't bring my harmonica, he thought. We could have had our duet. . . .

"Hi, Anne-Marie!"

Although she was early, Anne-Marie came racing up without turning a single cartwheel. "Buddy!" she called. "The most wonderful thing!" She had reached him now, and she seized his arm. "We're going away!" she said. "I came to say good-by."

"Where are you going?" asked Jimmy. "Into town for the day?"

"South America!" said Anne-Marie. "Brazil!" She was spinning around him now in a circle of racing cartwheels, and Jimmy had to keep turning to hear her. "All those Spanish lessons!" she was saying. "Now I must learn Portuguese — they speak Portuguese in Brazil."

"When are you going?" asked Jimmy. "On Tuesday, when the show closes?"

"Tonight!" Anne-Marie collapsed on the grass. "Papa got permission from the ringmaster, because our boat sails tomorrow night and it's a contract for all winter and Mama needs a day in New York to shop!" Jimmy opened his mouth to ask a question, but Anne-Marie didn't give him a chance.

"We are not the only ones!" she went on. "The performing dogs are going too, and somebody else — oh, yes — that nasty man with the nice little elephant." She jumped up. "Now I must go and tell Uncle James and Mr. Finlay and the Pierces, and then help Mama to pack our things."

As she darted through the door of the Seven Wonders tent, Jimmy suddenly realized what he had been told.

Brazil . . . South America . . . Mr. Sykes was taking Rex to South America!

Chapter Twenty-Five. A TRUCKFUL OF TIGERS

SOUTH AMERICA!" gasped Jimmy, bursting through the trailer door. "Sykes! He's taking Rex away tonight!"

Fred looked up from the blue wig he was combing. "Not tonight," he said calmly. "Tomorrow."

"But Anne-Marie said —"

"Sit down," said Fred. "Mrs. Dumont may have shopping to do in New York. Rex doesn't — and apparently Sykes doesn't, either. He has train reservations for tomorrow morning."

"What difference does that make?" asked Jimmy. "Tonight or tomorrow?"

"Lots of difference!" said Fred. He draped the wig over his fist and held it out at arms' length to examine it. "If Sykes is leaving tomorrow, we'll just have to make sure that Rex leaves tonight!" He hung the wig over a wooden block on the dressing table and swung round. "I think I know how we can do it, too!"

Jimmy sank down on the bunk. The panicky feeling was gone, now. If Fred had an idea — "But how will we

get Rex away from the grounds without anyone's see-
ing?" he asked. "And who told you that Sykes and the
Dumonts were leaving?"

"I hear things!" said Fred. "For instance, did you know
that the lion trainer, Mr. Fitz, is going to have lions *and*
tigers next year?"

"No," said Jimmy. "That's nice, I guess. But what
about Rex?"

"It takes a lot of time to train tigers," Fred went on,
dreamily. "Maybe that's why Mr. Fitz is having them
delivered here, tonight. Then they'll have a few days to
get used to him, and by the time he gets them down to
winter quarters in Florida, he'll be able to start training
them right away."

Jimmy was beginning to understand. "Tonight?" he
said.

"That's right," Fred nodded. "A big truck will drive
up, loaded with tigers. A little later it will drive away —"

"Loaded with elephant!" said Jimmy. "Loaded with me
and Rex! Oh, Fred, do you think we can work it?"

"I don't see why not," said Fred. "With luck, that is.
Now, the tigers will be delivered after midnight —"

"Why so late?" asked Jimmy.

"I don't know. Maybe the daytime crowds would make
them nervous and hard to handle. Or maybe the man just
can't get here any sooner! Now, when they're all unloaded, Mr. Fitz will probably take the driver to his place
for coffee and cake. Mrs. Fitz is making a special cake, so

he'll have to! You and Rex will be back of the tents in Animal Alley. I'll signal when the coast is clear, and the two of you can scoot aboard the truck. Okay?"

"It sounds fine," said Jimmy. "But what about Sykes?"

"There's a big poker game in Trailer Three," said Fred. "Should be a late one, too. I'm sure his dear friends will try to win all his money before he goes away! Was that the bell for lunch?"

It was hard to go through the day, knowing that it was his last with the show and unable to tell anyone about it. He might have told Anne-Marie, but when she said good-by after lunch, she was too full of the Dumonts' plans to think of anyone else's. "Uncle James will look after the things we leave behind," she told Jimmy. "Some he will sell, and some he will store away for us. It breaks Mama's heart to leave her beautiful stove. But I must go now. Papa is waiting to give me my first lesson in Portuguese. Sometimes I wish that my clever father did not speak ten languages! Good-by, Buddy!"

At supper Jimmy thought, "This is my last meal in the mess tent!" Everyone knew him now, and when friend after friend said "Hi, Buddy!" he suddenly realized that after tonight he wouldn't be Buddy any more. He would be Jimmy!

The last makeup job . . . He was getting pretty good at painting his face and putting on the false nose. The last entrance of the Fat Clown . . . As he listened to the

laughter of the crowd, when he fell on his back, he remembered the first time he had fallen. How frightened he
had been! It was too bad he had to leave now. Then the
elephant act came on and he remembered *why* he was
leaving.

Sykes no longer cared whether Fred stole his audience.
He had his contract for the whole winter. Twice he hit
Rex when he didn't move fast enough, and on his way out,
he stopped beside Fred to say, "In forty-eight hours we'll
be out of the country, Mr. Meddlesome Clown! From
now on I can treat this brute the way he deserves!" He
flourished his whip under Fred's nose, then turned on his
heel and marched out.

Jimmy clenched his fists. "I'll save you, Rex!" he mut-

tered under his breath. "Just another couple of hours and he'll never be able to touch you again!"

The tiger truck pulled into the grounds at half-past one. Jimmy and Fred saw it stop, and then withdrew for a last whispered conference.

"You know what to do?" asked Fred.

"I'll bring Rex around behind the wild animal tent, and wait there till you whistle," said Jimmy.

"Remember our signals?" asked Fred. "What's this?" He whistled a snatch of tune.

"All Clear," said Jimmy.

"And this one?" He whistled another.

"That's Danger," said Jimmy.

"Good," said Fred. "You know, it's too bad you have to go. I just thought of a wonderful routine with balloons under your costume instead of pillows. I'd have the long pin, and you would suddenly get very thin . . . I'll miss you, Buddy. Drop me a line sometime. Good Luck!" Before Jimmy could say a word, he had melted into the darkness and was gone.

When Rex saw Jimmy he shuffled his feet and made rumbling noises deep in his chest and picked him up and wouldn't let him go. "It's all right, boy!" Jimmy told him, hugging the familiar gray trunk. "I won't go away again. You can put me down!" But Rex paid no attention. It wasn't until Jimmy said, "Apples, Rex! I've got apples for you!" that Rex set him on the ground and started feeling his pockets. He found two apples and a bran muffin left over from supper, and while he ate Jimmy sawed away with his pocket knife at the heavy rope around Rex's leg. Then — "Up, boy!" he said. Perched once more on his pet's neck, he gently tugged the edge of one gray ear. "Here we go!" he said happily. "Quiet, now — this way, Rex!"

He had almost forgotten how quietly Rex could go. Guided by Jimmy's feet, he moved like a shadow between the dark blots of trailers and white ghosts of tents, sure-footed among tent-ropes and buckets that Jimmy couldn't see at all, until they came to Animal Alley.

The Alley was restless tonight. From every tent came growling or whinnying or rustling and stamping noises. When Jimmy stopped Rex behind the wild animal tent, the elephant shuffled and swayed uneasily. He, too, was disturbed by the nearness of the snarling tigers on the other side of the canvas wall, and it took all Jimmy's patting and whispered reassurances to keep him quiet.

Light glowed through the canvas, and Jimmy and Rex could see the square silhouettes of cages, and the shapes of moving men. At last the light went out, and Jimmy, tensed for action, waited for Fred's whistle.

But suppose the whistle didn't come, he thought suddenly. Suppose, instead, he heard a truck motor starting — a truck driving away? Suppose . . . ? Low and clear, Fred's whistle came through the night. The men had gone off towards Mr. Fitz's trailer, and the coast was clear.

"Now, Rex!" said Jimmy. The back of the truck was still open, a gaping, solid blackness that made the outdoors look almost light by comparison. Even Jimmy could smell the strong tiger odor as he urged the reluctant Rex through the opening. "All the way back!" said Jimmy. "He mustn't see us when he comes to close the door!"

Reluctantly, Rex shuffled forward, until — "Rex!" said Jimmy. "Stop! Something is moving back there! Look at all those eyes!"

Chapter Twenty-Six. EYES

B EHIND them was Animal Alley, and in front three pairs of gleaming eyes! If Jimmy and Rex left the truck now, they would surely be caught. The Alley was alive with the footsteps and flashlights of trainers, coming to look after their restless animals. No, they must stay where they were. They must travel as far as the truck would carry them — but travel *with what?*

Three pairs of eyes — tigers' eyes? But Mr. Fitz had already unloaded his animals. These must be for another circus. So Jimmy and Rex would have to travel in a dark, closed truck with three wild tigers! Of course they must be in cages, but suppose, somewhere on the road, a cage door was jolted open! Suddenly Rex began to move forward again.

"Rex!" said Jimmy. "I thought you were afraid of tigers!" Only a moment before, the mere smell of the tiger truck had disturbed Rex, and now he was advancing eagerly towards the eyes, which were flitting about in a most untigerlike manner. One pair bounded from the floor to the roof, another pair moved across to join the first, then all three darted to the center and hung, apparently in midair, staring at Jimmy and Rex.

Suddenly Jimmy's eyes were able to make out small, dim shapes behind a big mesh screen. "Monkeys!" he said, almost laughing with relief. "Don't get your trunk too close, Rex. They might pinch you!"

Nobody at the circus had ordered monkeys, or Fred would have known about it. Traveling with monkeys might be fun!

Outside, someone started to whistle. It was Fred. But instead of the All Clear, he was whistling their Danger signal!

The whistling came closer and closer. Right beside the truck it stopped, and Fred spoke. "Hello!" he said. "Is the poker game over already?"

Poker game! Then it must be — Jimmy pressed his ear to the side of the truck.

"My elephant!" snarled Sykes. "Somebody stole my elephant!"

"Are you sure?" asked Fred.

"The brute's gone!" said Sykes. "I wouldn't even have known if the animals hadn't been kicking up such a row! I came out to make sure that mine was behaving himself, and he was gone. The rope's cut!"

"He probably broke it himself," said Fred. "I'll bet we'll find him eating hay over by the animal exhibits building, or maybe at the fruit stand near the west gate. Come on — I'll help you find him."

Sykes seemed suspicious. "You're very helpful all of a sudden!" he said.

"I don't want to see the poor beast get into trouble," Fred's voice was moving away now. "We can try the west gate first."

Sykes' voice followed, muttering threats, and Jimmy drew a deep breath. If Fred could just keep Sykes out of the way until . . .

"My hat!" bellowed Sykes. "Where did that monkey come from? Come back, you devil!"

Monkey? thought Jimmy. He turned toward the cage. "Oh, Rex!" he said. Once again — and once too often — Rex had done his favorite trick, door opening. Now two hooks dangled empty, a bolt had been pulled back, and the door swung open. All the monkeys were gone.

At Jimmy's reproachful tone, Rex hung his head. "Do you *want* Sykes to take you to South America?" asked Jimmy. But it was too late for scolding now. Whoever caught the monkeys and put them back would find Rex in the truck — *unless* Jimmy and Fred could put them away first!

"Stay here!" he told Rex. "Stay here, and try to behave yourself." He managed to slip from the truck without getting caught in the crisscrossing flashlight beams of the monkey hunters. Most of them seemed to be from Sykes's poker party.

"Here!" Fred thrust a monkey into Jimmy's hands. "Put it back!"

Jimmy locked the monkey in its cage, told Rex, "Leave that door alone" — and ran out again.

He found Fred arguing with a very large stevedore who had caught the second monkey and insisted on putting it away himself. "Where's the cage?" he asked. "I caught it, and I'll — what's going on over there?"

Over by the tents, a bellow from Sykes had been followed by a roar of laughter from the other men. "He's got Sykes's whip!" someone yelled. "Hey, Sykes, what are you going to do without your whip?"

"Here!" said the stevedore. He thrust the monkey into Fred's hands and hurried towards the tents.

Fred passed the squirming monkey to Jimmy, who ran to shut it away in the cage. Again he warned Rex, and then hurried out again to join in the pursuit of the third monkey. If only they could get that one put away before the truck driver came back!

But the last monkey was in no hurry to be caught. He swarmed up ropes, and slid down tent roofs, and played hide-and-seek behind water buckets, always just out of reach. Then he disappeared and they thought they had lost him, until one of the roving flashlights picked him up high on the center pole of a tent. He was wearing Mr. Sykes's hat, and trying to tie the whip around his waist.

"Looks more like old Sykes in that hat than Sykes does," called one of the men.

"Come down!" shouted Sykes. He picked up a stone

and threw it at the monkey, who chattered and jumped and threw down Sykes's hat. It landed in a tub of dirty water. Then, dazzled by the flashlights, the monkey rubbed his eyes, pitched the whip out into the darkness, and turned and slid down one of the tent ropes — right into the hands of Sykes's friend, the merry-go-round man's helper.

"I'll take him!" said Fred, but Sykes got there first.

"Steal from me, will you?" Sykes shook the monkey. "I'll teach you — I'll twist your tail until — Ouch! He bit me!" After that he didn't try to twist the monkey's tail again, but, holding it at arms' length, he still insisted on locking it up himself.

Jimmy and Fred could do nothing, as Sykes climbed into the truck, clutching the chattering, squirming monkey and muttering threats. The crowd had drifted away as soon as the monkey was caught, and now only the merry-go-round man's helper was left, lounging against the truck with a cigarette hanging from his lower lip, as he waited for Sykes.

"Hey!" cried Sykes, inside the truck. "Hiding here, are you? You just wait!" The door of the monkey cage clanged shut. "Now! Run away from me, will you?" Fred clutched Jimmy's shoulder as Sykes emerged from the truck, half leading and half dragging a reluctant Rex.

Once outside, however, Rex balked. Perhaps the sight of Jimmy gave him courage. He set his four feet on the ground and refused to budge. Sykes was white with fury.

"Get funny with me, will you? Run away, and then get funny! My whip! Where did that monkey drop it? Well, I'll find it, and until I do — " He gave Rex's tail a vicious tweak. Rex squealed with pain, and, at the sound, Jimmy's restraint snapped.

He had always been careful not to let Sykes hear his voice, but now he ran forward shouting, "You big bully! You leave Rex alone!"

"The McLean brat!" Sykes had Jimmy by the arm, but when he looked at him he was so surprised that his anger seemed to have vanished. "No — it's the kid clown! . . . So *that's* it!"

"Take the elephant!" Sykes told his friend. "Tie him up. I'll attend to *him* later!"

The fellow from the merry-go-round stood staring, his mouth half open. "What about the game?" he said.

"Tie the brute up, and then you can go back to the game. Tell them I'll be along later. *We* have business here!" He had Jimmy by the collar now, and was dragging him along. When Fred tried to help, Sykes said, "*You're* going to jail, clown, for stealing an elephant, and hiding a runaway boy — and if you touch me, I'll charge you with assault, too! But first I'm going to call our old friends, the Mudges. If only I had my whip!"

"You wouldn't dare!" said Fred. Sykes laughed, and gave Jimmy a shake. Behind them, Jimmy heard the truck motor starting. Mr. Fitz and the driver must have come back. Their last chance was going to drive away!

"So long!" called Mr. Fitz's voice. "Sorry you won't stay the rest of the night."

"I'm in a hurry!" a cheerful voice called back. "I've got a boy at home I haven't seen for nearly two months."

With a sudden twist, Jimmy freed himself from Sykes's grasp and ran toward the truck. "Dad!" he shouted. "Dad — it's Jimmy! I'm here!"

The motor stopped. Sykes had Jimmy by the collar again and was shaking him, and Fred was pulling at Sykes's arm, and then suddenly Jimmy was free and Sykes was being shaken till his head wobbled.

"What — are — you — doing — to my boy?" said Mr. McLean, grimly.

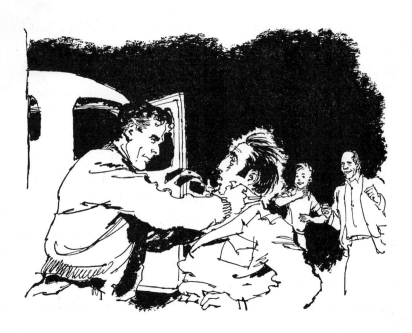

Chapter Twenty-Seven. A TOAST TO
THE FUTURE

IT WAS three o'clock in the morning. The police car had just driven away with Mr. Sykes. ("Don't let him forget his whip, officer!" Fred had said. "Here — I found it for him. He was going to do awful things with that whip!") Now Jimmy, Fred, and Mr. McLean were having a very late supper, or early breakfast, in Fred's trailer. They had left the door open, and from time to time Rex poked his head in for Jimmy to pat his trunk and feed him things.

"I caught an early boat," Mr. McLean was explaining. "I hurried with my business because I wanted to get home early, and have a week with Jimmy before he went back to school. I very nearly phoned home when I landed."

"It's a good thing you didn't!" said Jimmy. "The Mudges would have told Mr. Sykes. The Mudges! Won't they be surprised when we all come home together — you, and Rex, and me!"

Mr. McLean put his arm around Jimmy's shoulder. "We'll take care of the Mudges!" he said. "Luckily, I decided to get rid of the animals in a hurry and then go home and surprise you. Those tigers were my second-last delivery. I just have some monkeys now."

"We know!" said Jimmy. Fred laughed, and then Mr. McLean had to hear all about Rex's door-opening trick and the monkey chase in the dark.

The story and the food were finished at the same time, and Fred said, "You'll stay the rest of the night, Mr. McLean? The next few days are going to be pretty lonesome for me without Buddy — I mean, Jimmy! I'm sorry you won't have a chance to see him work in the ring, too. He has the makings of a fine clown."

"It's up to Jimmy," said Mr. McLean. "I'll deliver the monkeys in the morning. They go to a zoo not far from here. After that, my time is his. If he wants to stay until the show closes, it's all right with me. Would I see Rex work too?"

"Rex!" said Jimmy. Rex popped his head through the door; he thought he was being called. But for once Jimmy didn't notice him. "Sykes is gone!" Jimmy said. "Do you think — could Rex and I —"

Fred laughed. "My act is growing!" he said. "First a boy, and now an elephant! I'll speak to the ringmaster first thing in the morning. Now, how about a couple of hours' sleep?"

He yawned, and stretched, and made a funny face, but Jimmy didn't even notice. "A clown," he said. "An elephant clown. I wonder if the audience will like it?"

"We'll soon find out!" said Fred.

Ten hours later, the audience itself answered the question. They laughed when Rex, wearing a silly little clown hat, tapped Fred on the shoulder and frightened him into a double somersault. They clapped when the fat clown who was Jimmy put him through a few of the tricks he had learned in the schoolyard at home. And when Rex picked Jimmy up by one leg, and refused to let him down in spite of his struggles, the audience laughed and clapped so hard that the ringmaster signaled for them to do more tricks. They did; but first Jimmy made Rex bow toward one of the front boxes where Mr. McLean sat, laughing and clapping harder than anybody else in the tent.

That night they made the act still longer, and on Monday and Tuesday Rex did every trick he knew.

Mr. McLean had invited all Jimmy's friends to a farewell party on Tuesday night, so after the last performance they gathered at the trailer of Mr. Finlay, the giant, which was the only one big enough to hold everybody. It was certainly the only one big enough to hold Mr. Finlay! There were nine kinds of sandwiches and gallons of lemonade, and the merry-go-round man brought a bushel basket full of pink popcorn. He set it down just inside the door — and that was a mistake!

Rex couldn't come in to the party, of course, but he poked his head in every few minutes, and when he saw the pink popcorn he sampled it, liked it — and half-emptied the basket before he was caught.

Jimmy had brought his harmonica, and he and Mr. Finlay played a duet, "There's a Long, Long Trail A-Wind-ing." While everyone was clapping and saying how good they were, Mr. McLean took the harmonica. "I wonder if I can still play one of these things?" he said.

Jimmy was a little worried — everyone was watching — but Mr. McLean ran up and down the scale a few times and then burst into "The Road to Mandalay." He was so good that people started singing, and when he had to stop for breath, Jimmy said, "You never told me you could play a harmonica!"

"You never asked me!" said Mr. McLean.

"I think you're even better than Charley!" Jimmy de-clared.

"That's your gas-station friend, isn't it?" said Mr. Mc-Lean. "We'll find out when we get to his place tomorrow. I'm looking forward to meeting him, and his aunt, and your Tigers and Kangaroos — and we'll see the Dixons, too. Come in, Ringmaster! Have some lemonade and a sandwich! How do you like having an elephant for a clown?"

The ringmaster took a large bite of sandwich. "Won-derful!" he said, his mouth full of rye bread and corned beef. "Wonderful! But why did it have to start at the end of the season? Next summer," he said, waving his sand-wich, "we'll start right at the beginning, with pictures on all the posters. You are coming back next year, aren't you?"

This was something Jimmy hadn't even dared to dream about. To travel all summer with the show — to go from town to town with Rex and all his circus friends — "Can I, Dad?" He looked anxiously at his father.

"Rex is a natural clown!" the ringmaster, still talking, was already eating his third sandwich. "We could build a real act around him — a burning clown-house, with Rex pulling a little fire engine and squirting water on the fire and all over the other clowns."

Water! There was nothing Rex liked better than playing with water. If only his father would let them go! Every one was waiting, now, to hear what Mr. McLean would say. He wasn't smiling.

"I — don't know," said Mr. McLean. "If I could travel with him — but I have to go away again next summer, and I want to be sure he's properly settled and taken care of this time."

"I can take care of myself!" protested Jimmy. "I'll be thirteen!"

"He can travel with me," said Fred. "After all, he and Rex are part of my act."

"And I'll keep an eye on both of them!" piped Mrs. Pierce, whose chin just showed over the edge of the giant's table, even though she was sitting on two large books and a cushion. "I'll make him behave, and the elephant too!" She sounded so fierce that everyone laughed, but still they looked at Mr. McLean. Suddenly, he seemed to make up his mind. He smiled and stood up. But instead of answering Jimmy, he said, "Lemonade, everybody! Please fill your glasses for a toast!"

When all the glasses were filled, Mr. McLean raised his own and said, "Let's drink to — Reunion next summer!"

"Next summer!" said Mr. Finlay and Mrs. Kincaid and the Pierces, raising their glasses and drinking.

"Next summer!" said the ringmaster, and Uncle James, and the merry-go-round man.

"Next summer!" said Fred. "To Jimmy, Rex, and Fred, the Comedy Clowns, in the funniest act in history!" He drank, and then said, "Jimmy, where's the bucket? Let's give Rex some lemonade so he can drink that toast too!"